FOUR SEASONS OF HORROR

KRISTAL SHANAHAN

Book cover art: Grim Poppy Design
Editor: Marked Up Editing
Ebook and Interior Format: Steven Pajak

Trade Paperback ISBN: ISBN: 979-8-9913380-4-2

"Temptation is the devil looking through the keyhole. Yielding is opening the door and inviting him in."

— BILLY SUNDAY

PART ONE
SUMMER

OCEAN DWELLERS

Driving with the top down, rock music blasting, and the wind in their hair was pure bliss. The sun was out with the eighty degree heat beating down on their sunkissed faces and shoulders. Scenic Big Sur along Highway One was a beautiful drive with an endless Pacific Ocean view of cliffs and valleys for miles. Heading out for their last trip for the summer would hopefully prove to be one to remember. James Hall and Morgan Barnes wanted nothing more than to have a great time and travel as often as their schedules allowed.

PULLING INTO A CAMPGROUND NEAR ONE OF THE cliffs, they parked at the office to pay for their time there. They only planned to stay two nights. After they grabbed supplies and paid, they drove to their campsite to set up. Morgan could only handle two nights of real camping before she felt completely disgusting. After they set up the tent, they blew up the air mattress and Morgan made the bed. They set up their table and chairs and travel grill. They made sure the food was secure in the containers so animals wouldn't get in them. After they had everything set up, they decided to make their way to the bluff after lunch. Eating typical camping food; burgers, chips, and fruit, proved to be filling and was quite good. Morgan and James relaxed and talked for a while after lunch. Their relationship was one built on friendship first and the banter between them was fun and constant. They weren't in a hurry to cliff dive and swim;

they wanted to enjoy each other's company for a couple of hours first.

THEY WALKED HAND IN HAND TOWARD THE BLUFF, both agreeing to jump together. The grass was sparse, the dirt dry, and the cliff was now visibly looming over the water. Peering over the cliff, the ocean below looked inviting, yet waves aggressively lapped at the rocks below. Morgan was a little apprehensive about jumping. Something didn't feel right. As adrenaline junkies, a summer goal included cliff jumping, and this would check off the last box before they would head back to college and start their junior year. Morgan looked over at James. He looked completely relaxed and happy. His blond hair, blue eyes, and deep tan made him easy on the eyes. She had the same features and both had athletic builds. People often referred to them as Ken and Barbie. While the comparison was nauseating, she understood that it sometimes was a compliment and sometimes, it wasn't.

She was terrified. She knew the risks, and James felt like nothing terrible would ever happen. Standing at the edge of the bluff and peering down at the blue endless depth below, the young couple felt empowered by what they were about to accomplish. The waves had slightly calmed and they knew the water was at least 15 feet deep. They researched the area before deciding to jump here. A few months ago they tandem jumped from a plane and that high would be tough to beat. Making sure that whatever adventure they took, they did what they could to ensure their safety. They looked at each other and prepared mentally for the descent.

They edged as close as they could for the jump. Gazing down at the water, Morgan thought she saw a large looming shadow beneath the surface. There wasn't supposed to be any sharks or any predatory gliding monsters under the water. She convinced herself that it must have been shadows playing tricks on her when the clouds moved in front of the sun.

"James, you ready?" Morgan asked with trepidation.

"Hell yeah! Let's do this. Love you."

James gave Morgan a quick kiss and squeezed her hand. They looked at each other and then they jumped. Not long after they jumped, they landed simultaneously in the ocean. Coming up a few seconds after the other, when they breached the water, they breathed deeply and searched for each other. When they found each other, they locked eyes and displayed grins wider than the

Grand Canyon. They swam toward each other and excitedly embraced.

"We did it!" Morgan squealed.

"I didn't doubt that we would." Laughing, James splashed Morgan.

They splashed back and forth for a moment until something caught James' attention.

"Hey, let's swim over there. It looks cool."

James pointed to a rocky area with climbable rocks for them to sit. They swam over there and pulled themselves up on the slick, mossy rocks to sun themselves and hang out for a bit. They laid out and rested while talking about the rest of their trip they had planned. The sun was still out with a slight breeze, and low 80s made for a perfect summer day. The sounds of water rushing and continuously hitting the rocks was hypnotic and serene.

"This place is really pretty." Morgan said, looking around.

"Yeah it is. I don't know how we got so lucky to be here alone." James said while looking at Morgan.

Below the surface, strange noises were becoming increasingly louder. Clicking sounds from underwater were consistent and relentless. Morgan and James sat up on the rocks, scared to move. The only way to get back across was to swim. Whatever was making those noises was under water, and they were unable to leave without encountering what was under the surface of the ocean. Breaking through the water slowly, were black, long, gnarly, giant subhuman hands with razor sharp nails. Reaching out of the water as far as it could to graze James' ankle, it sliced it open then disappeared under the water.

"What the hell!"

James jerked his legs up close to the center of the rock formation to look at his injury. It didn't appear that deep or needing stitches. He covered the wound with his hand to put pressure on it to stop the bleeding. He didn't have anything to put on it.

"James! What happened?"

Morgan expected to see a dorsal fin appear in the water, so she was distracted until James yelled out in pain.

"I, I–don't know. Cut my ankle somehow. Maybe I hit it on a sharp protruding piece of rock."

"Just keep your hand on it. I'll look around to see if I can see anything." Morgan replied.

Not seeing any protruding rock pieces or anything that would have cut James, Morgan became concerned. It came from somewhere.

"James, there isn't anything that could've done that, that I can see. I have no idea how that happened."

"The only explanation is something from the water

then. Maybe my foot was in the water. For now, we need to stay out of the water and hope that if something is down there, it goes away soon." James tried to sound as if he wasn't nearly as scared as he felt.

"Then we stay in the center here and not stretch back out. Surely whatever did that will move on." Morgan attempted to be the optimist as always.

After a couple of hours, Morgan and James were tired from the sun exposure and their throats were dry from no water. The opportunity for water was nonexistent and dehydration was likely soon if they didn't make it back to camp. Calm waters lapped the edges of the moss covered rocks they were perched on. Burnt, thirsty and tired, they were frustrated and scared to venture in the water of fear of what lay beyond the depths and beyond.

"Why don't I just get in for a minute and test the water to see if it's ok?" Morgan asked.

"I can't see how that would be a good idea Morgan. Let me test the water instead. My ankle stopped bleeding, so I'll be fine."

James scooted to the edge of the rock formation and slowly slid in the water next to the rocks.

"The water feels great, I think it's fine. Why don't you slide in for a minute to cool off."

Morgan looked skeptical, but nodded her head in agreement. She slid in carefully next to James. She sighed deeply from the relief of the constant sun beating down on them without the break of clouds. They didn't swim or move around much to avoid attention from whatever lay beneath. Morgan wanted to get back up on the rocks.

"I'm getting out, can you give me a boost since I'm tired?" Morgan asked.

"Yeah, go ahead, I got you." James gave her the help she needed.

Morgan was back on the rocks and felt safe in the middle and sat cross legged, hugging her legs to herself since it was the best way to make herself small without her extremities dangling into the ocean. She watched James below. He started to climb up so she moved to give him a hand. As James was pulling himself up, he abruptly lost his footing and went under the water. Morgan quickly crawled to the edge and looked over the rocks, screaming for James.

"James! Where are you? Give me your hand! James?" Morgan screamed for him for several minutes.

James emerged rushing up from underneath the water. Streams of red were surrounding him and Morgan reached down to grab him. She was able to help him up and he pulled himself up the rest of the way. They scooted toward the center of the rocks.

Weakly, James spoke, "There's something evil down there. I know I've lost a lot of blood."

Large rivers of blood were cascading down the rocks into the water. James' color drained from his face even though he was sunburned and his strength was waning due to all the blood loss. His right leg was shredded like ribbons. Sinew and bones protrude through the broken skin. Morgan hovered over him, weeping and feeling utterly helpless. She caressed his face and his hair, loving on him as much as she could. She was terrified she was going to lose him.

Inching down, the sun was setting and they were slowly losing hope of getting off the rocks. Morgan's goosebumps were prominent on her arms and legs. She had overwhelming fear take over her body and her mind. Unfortunately, they chose an isolated area that didn't have tourists or locals yet. It just happened to be an unseasonably warm day in June for their first vacation stop with no one to help for miles, and they left their phones at the campsite. Morgan was at a loss as to what to do. She was scared to go for help because whatever was down there, was likely to get her too. In essence, their time was running out.

"If you want to dive and swim for it, I don't blame you. Go for it. I'll still be here." James whispered, giving her hand a loving squeeze.

"You sure? I don't know if I can leave you." Morgan

choked up as she spoke to the man she loved more than anyone on the planet.

"Yeah, go." James encouraged her to go. He wanted her to save herself. No sense in both of them dying.

Morgan stood up cautiously and stood near the edge. She was an experienced swimmer and diver. She's been swimming since she was five and knew she was a quick swimmer and she was strong. Taking a leap of faith, she dove in head first. She swam for her life the short distance to the shore.

SHE PULLED HERSELF UP AND STARTED SCREAMING for help, running toward the camp site. The store was closed and they were the only ones staying that night. When she got back to their camp site after not having any luck at the office, she grabbed her phone from inside the tent. No cell service was popping up.

"Damn it!" She screamed as loudly as she could.

Grabbing a towel and putting shorts on, she clutched her phone in one hand and the towel in the other, and ran back to where James was stuck on the rock. As she approached, she realized it had gotten darker in the short time that she was gone. She held up her cell phone, hoping for service, but she wasn't able to get service here either. She looked at her battery life and the phone was nearly dead. She texted her mom telling her where they were and to send an ambulance because James was hurt and might not survive. Holding on to her phone, she held the towel in front of her face and screamed and cried into the towel, kneeling down while she sobbed for a moment. She needed that release and now she needed to be strong for James. She stood up and walked up to the water's edge, where she came from earlier. She turned the cell phone flashlight on and shined it toward James. It didn't help much as she couldn't see him. Her phone was waterproof so she tucked into her bikini top, hoping it would hold. She dropped the towel on the ground before her. She dove back in to save James.

Pulling herself up on the slippery rocks proved to be difficult due to no food or water, and sheer exhaustion. She sat back beside James and it was obvious he was barely hanging on.

"Hey, James, honey I'm here. I texted my mom, so hopefully help will be here soon. I still can't get service to call anywhere though. Morgan turned on her cell phone flashlight to look at his leg. It looked like processed meat that had gone bad. It was disgusting and she gagged. She had to turn away and retched off the side of the rocks. As she finished, soulless eyes were gazing hungrily into hers.

The largest, boniest hands, with the span of half her height reached up and stroked her body from the neck down. It had no eyes, just an endless black depth where the sockets were. The enormous mouth housed razor sharp teeth that made any great white shark look infantile. The sinister smile was wide and gaping. It could inhale her in two bites, and he looked hungry. The slick darkened skin lent itself to the evil that crawled up from unknown depths of hell.

The skin ripper wasn't done with James. It enjoyed its prey helpless, but still alive to evoke the terror that it elicits and craves. Depredation was near. Morgan tried to escape, but with one swipe, she was immoble and incapacitated. The creature slinked its way over to James and towered over him. Bit by bit, the skin ripper began to rip strips of skin off of James, starting with his untouched leg. Every skin ribbon torn from James' body, the creature devoured as if it was snacking before the main entree. Once it was done with his legs, he moved to his torso and ripped pieces of skin off and devoured every one of them he took from James. It made clicking noises and then it picked up James with one hand and put his head and half his body in its mouth, and the crunching of James' body could be heard by Morgan as she woke up and saw that James was ripped in half. She whimpered quietly. The monster threw the rest of James in its mouth and swallowed it whole. James was gone.

Madison looked at the creature in disbelief. It was surreal that this was her reality. It injured her so terribly she couldn't move. She knew her fate would be the same as James'. The skin ripper jumped back in the water and then everything became eerily still. Morgan knew that she wouldn't have long to wait for its return. The claws had torn her back and the bleeding was pooling around her faster than anticipated. She tried to move to see if she could make it to shore, but her body wouldn't cooperate. Grabbing her cell phone, which was within arms' length from the rock where she dropped it, she looked to see if there were bars on the phone to show any amount of service. She didn't have any luck. It looked like her text to her mom went through at least. She texted her mom that that an ocean creature ate him and she was about to suffer the same fate. She knew how fucking crazy that sounds.

Mom, I love you and dad more than life itself. Please tell James' parents that we love them too.

The creature slowly ascended from the depths of the ocean for its second course. Morgan thought maybe she could reason with it. It likely was an intelligent evil creature.

"Please, please leave me alone!

You took James from me, don't take me too!"

She pleaded as best as she could. Crying, she began to plead again for her life, knowing deep down it didn't matter. Tears streamed down her face as she tried one more time.

"Please, s–" She screamed, in excruciating pain.

The skin ripper started to strip her skin off like it did to James. The process was the same for Morgan, so she knew what would happen to her. She was losing consciousness as the pain was more than she could bear. Being eaten alive by a creature that wasn't even known to exist, simply wasn't fathomable.

Suddenly, hissing could be heard from the water. The skin ripper stopped and was motionless for a few seconds and turned its head to the direction of the sounds. It stood up and looked down to the darkness beyond the visible eye, into the ocean. Seconds later, another creature just like the one towering over its prey climbed up on the rocks. They began to hiss and click at each other. The one over Morgan swiped at the new one, and gouged its chest open. Green ooze slowly leaked out. They continued to fight. The one that had been eating Morgan picked her up and ripped her in half. The other creature took the rest of her and devoured her lower half in seconds.

Sirens could be heard in the distance, nearing the bluff where the skin rippers stood. Communicating with each other through clicks and hisses, they jumped back in the ocean. All that remained on the rocks were both fresh and dried blood stains under Morgan's phone. Lurking just below the surface near the rocks, the skin rippers waited.

CLARA KNOWS POSSESSION

PROLOGUE

Running through the deserted carnival midway, Dawn couldn't escape from the force pulling at her backside, trying to stop her. With terror-stricken eyes and falling prey to the unseen malevolent force, she felt a chill as rain moved in alongside what she was fighting. Thunder rumbled and lightning lit up the darkened clouds hovering over the midway. Dawn continued to run until the midway came to an abrupt end. She stopped, turned around, and as lightning struck the sky again, she was forced to look at the evil presence before her. She didn't quite look human as she gazed at Dawn with hunger in her eyes and a stance that was quickly replaced with a leap towards Dawn.

Dawn stumbled back and hit the ground hard. Straddling Dawn with an unmatched strength, the ghostly entity entered Dawn's body quickly and violently. Dawn screamed and rolled over to vomit. She was confused about what just happened, but dusted herself off and slowly stood up. Not feeling quite herself or in control of her own body, she walked towards one of the trailers that the carnies live in.

The carnival is visiting a typical small town in the midwest and has one more day until they pack it all up and move on to the next town. Dawn knocked on the door and waited until a man that had apparently been asleep answered the door.

"Dawn? What the hell do you want? Can't ya see I'm sleepin?"

"I wanted to give you a chance to say you're sorry for what you did yesterday." Dawn spoke in a calm and monotonous voice.

"I didn't do a damn thing bitch, now get outta here!"

"So Dan, does that mean that our time spent together meant nothing to you?"

"A few hours of fun was all you meant to me. Now, just go away Dawn."

"I just can't do that Dan, Sharon would be so upset with me if I were to just let it go."

Dan was gruff and disheveled, but quickly turned ten shades of white and slammed the door in her face. Banging her forehead on the door multiple times drew blood that ran down her face. Controlling herself proved impossible.

"Go away or I'll call the police!" Dan spoke with fear in his voice.

Dawn was confused about what to do next. Leaning against the now dented, blood smeared door, she slowly stumbled back and headed back towards the way she came down the midway. Dawn wanted to go home, but her thoughts were muddled by the ghost that inhabited her body. Methodically walking towards an area where stuffed animals and dolls populated the midway en masse, Dawn stopped to gaze at a beautiful but haunting porcelain doll.

Dawn asked Sharon, "I have an idea. How 'bout you get inside that pretty doll and tomorrow when a little girl wins it, you can inhabit her, and stay a while in her body and maybe grow up as her, or whoever wins it?"

Dawn was willing to say whatever necessary so she could escape. Hoping she chose the right location and plan for Sharon, she continued to look at the doll.

Dawn collapsed on the ground in front of the dolls and stuffed animals. Sharon's spirit escaped her as an overwhelming feeling of exhaustion enveloped her as she peered up at Sharon and watched her work her way into the doll. The doll appeared to shudder and slightly rock, and then all was still. Breathing a sigh of relief, Dawn carefully stood up, and ran towards her car so she could get home. She vowed to never go to another carnival or mess around with a carnie again.

THIRTY YEARS LATER...

Dusty surfaces and long forgotten objects littered the shelves of the toy and antique store, *Harbor Curiosities*. Dim lighting created an ambiance of unnatural and eerie items for sale, luring hopeful bargain hunters searching for their treasure. Antiques have littered the shelves in this store since the 1970s. Some items have been on the shelves for that long, collecting dust. The owner inherited the store from her parents and is unaware of the pasts that some collectibles possess. Several shelves are also dedicated to new and old toys and games which sell well at times, especially during the holidays.

Arriving at the antique store on a Saturday morning, Annie and her mom were shopping with nothing in particular in mind. Perusing the aisles with an abundance of relics at eye level, Annie spotted a beautiful porcelain doll. As Kristi looked at it, a feeling of unease overcame her.

"Annie, let's keep looking. There are tons of undiscovered vintage or cool toys here, I'm sure of it."

"Mom, it's beautiful! Just look at her. She has red hair, just like me!"

"Annie, why don't you hold her as we walk around, and if you see something you like better, you can put her back." Kristi hoped she would put the doll back. *Surely, there's something else here,* she thought.

Kristi continued to peer at the doll with trepidation. It had a likening to her daughter, with the fiery red hair and porcelain skin. The carefully curated outfit was unlike anything she had ever seen on a doll before. A knit vest with other unique and striking features completed the look of the one-of-a-kind creation. The doll was beautiful; she just wanted it to stay in the store and far away from them.

Truth be told, Kristi had always had an unfettered fear of anything resembling clowns or creepy dolls in general; they made her uncomfortable, and she couldn't quite figure out why. Annie had picked it up and was staking her claim on the doll as if she had possessed it her entire life. Kristi sighed because she knew she would buy that damn doll for Annie. Her daughter held it like her life depended on it.

Making their way throughout the store, Annie saw nothing else she wanted. They headed towards the register so they could pay for the doll. Handing over $80.00 felt like paying a small fortune for it. If Kristi didn't know better, she would've thought the cashier was happy to see the doll go. When they got in the car, she had never seen Annie so happy. Maybe it was worth it to get the doll. Shoving her conflicted feelings down, she decided to embrace her daughter's happiness. Sighing, she started the car, and they headed home. From the backseat, Annie was whispering to the doll. She seemed to zone out for a minute and then snap out of it.

"Mom, I'm naming her Clara. It just fits, you know?"

"Sure, honey, that's a great name."

"I can't wait to show my friends. I'm sure they will think she's pretty, too!"

With a forced laugh, "I'm sure they will be jealous they don't have their own Clara."

"Yeah, they will be soooo jealous!" Annie spoke with a twinkle in her eyes and excitement in her voice.

LOOKING OUT HER BEDROOM WINDOW, ANNIE SAW her neighborhood friends outside. The August sun spread warmth from the window to Annie's palms as she laid them flush against the window. Closing her eyes and letting the warmth from the window warm her hands and her soul. Embracing the simple joys in life was important to her, even as a young girl. She was the youngest of the kids that played together. Most of the neighborhood kids were thirteen or fourteen, but they always included Annie, even though Annie was only twelve. Wanting to join them and show off her doll, she grabbed Clara from her bed and stumbled back while clutching the doll tightly. Weird visions plagued her mind, and she didn't understand what was happening. Wondering why she saw a woman running from something in her thoughts, she looked at Clara. Shaking her head to clear her thoughts, she ran downstairs to join her friends.

Placing Clara safely on the porch swing, she ran across the street to join the kickball game already in progress. It was boys against girls. The others moved the game into the street while Annie grabbed a piece of chalk from her bucket of toys on the porch. She marked the goals on the street for both teams. Each goal was a point to keep it simple. This was their version of kickball, not really knowing the true rules of the sport they often played. After Annie finished the goal lines, Brian stuck his foot out and tripped her. She fell, catching herself with her palms. A light breeze swept through, making the burning of her palms easier to bear as she clambered to sit up.

Brian had a smirk on his face, "Oops, sorry there, Annie. I didn't see you."

"Right. Okay, Brian." Annie gave him a dirty look and walked across the street where the girls were, rubbing her palms to lessen the sting. She looked back at Brian, fuming on the inside. They locked eyes and Annie stood her ground until Brian broke his stare and turned.

Brian walked over to where the boys stood together. Jake, one of the other neighborhood boys, said, "Hey Brian, that was a real dick move. Annie is really sweet and a couple of years younger than you. Why would you fucking do that?"

"I don't know, I just felt like it. She's got that creepy doll over there and it just bugs me. I feel like it's been staring at me since they came outside. I know how crazy that sounds. Something just came over me. It's like I couldn't control myself."

A stark wind picked up again as they were about to start the game. Brian lost his balance as he was about to kick the ball. He stumbled backwards and hit his head on the curb. Brian was splayed out on the street with blood pooling around his head, causing his friends to grow silent. They gasped as they looked on in horror. Brian's mom came outside when she heard the commotion.

"What happened?" Mrs. Asher asked the kids as she looked down and noticed her son. She screamed and collapsed on the ground. Her screams continued and drew neighbors out of their homes.

Kristi came outside, saw Brian, and rushed inside to call 9-1-1. Afterwards, she ran back out over to Lydia Asher with a towel in her hands.

"Lydia, I called 9-1-1. They will be here in a couple of minutes. We need to see if we can stop the bleeding by putting pressure on his head."

Lydia was trying to revive him with CPR, yet Brian's body was limp and lifeless every time she gave compressions. "Brian, it's mom. Can you hear me? Brian, please say something. Please, please, Brian, SAY SOMETHING!" She screamed in anguish and despair, then sobbed while cradling Brian's head. She was lost in her grief and didn't hear the sirens approach the neighborhood.

Kristi was crouched down next to Brian, staring at Lydia with the most helpless feeling she'd ever had. He was pale as a ghost and unresponsive every time Lydia tried to get him to wake up. His head lolled to the side and his eyes were wide open and glassy, frozen in a look of horror. Kristi closed his eyes while trying to hide her tears, but they gave her away as the kids looked on.

"Annie, you and your friends go inside and grab snacks and watch a movie in the living room. You don't need to be out here."

Annie nodded her head, "Okay mom."

Brian's friends hung their heads in sadness and despair. Disappearing inside Annie's home as the para-medics arrived, they headed to the kitchen out of habit.

The paramedics and police were talking to Lydia and Kristi. They did their best to revive Brian, but he was already gone when they got there. After questioning them and determining that it was an accident, Lydia looked on while the paramedics zipped her only child up in the black body bag. She was numb and collapsed again on her perfectly manicured yard. Her body shook as she sobbed alone.

ALL THE KIDS JUST STOOD AROUND THE KITCHEN, not knowing what to do, and looked uncomfortable after the death of their friend. Annie's mom had set out lemonade and cookies on the kitchen table, so the kids naturally gravitated there. Sitting down and enjoying the cookies and the lemonade, the kids sat in the still, depressive silence, for a few minutes. Jake was the first to speak.

"So that was weird that Brian fell over and hit his head, huh?" Jake asked the group in a whisper.

"I mean, it's like karma, you know? He hurt Annie, and he fell down. He deserved it," said Steph. She seemed surprised at herself for sounding so cruel.

"I don't know about that." Jake said while he was running his hands along the wooden table. "Ouch!" He yelled.

A splinter was protruding from his thumb. He felt like someone had taken a knife to his hand, but none of his friends were paying attention to him. They were engrossed in a couple of side conversations. He looked at Annie's doll, remembering what Brian had said, and thought he saw a slight turn of its head. He shivered.

The neighborhood kids finished their snacks and were getting ready to go home. The overwhelming afternoon had left the kids exhausted.

Annie spoke softly, "See you guys tomorrow? Last day

before school starts." She picked up Clara and went upstairs.

Jake, Steph, and Amanda all looked at each other after Annie left.

"Anyone else find that doll creepy as hell? I can't believe that her mom got that for her." Steph was waiting for a response from the others.

"Yeah, I find it weird. I mean, Annie is going into 6th grade and she's still playing with dolls." Jake was laughing at his own comment, and the girls joined in. From the second floor, Annie heard them laughing at her expense.

Annie was listening at the top of the stairs, hidden from her friends' view. Their voices carried toward Annie. Tears streamed down her face as she sat, quietly crying.

Amanda tried to speak in a hushed tone, "So I heard the doll was bought at a creepy antique store about an hour outside of town. Her mom freaked out when they got home with it. I think she had flashbacks of something that happened a long time ago. That's what my mom said, anyway. She called my mom afterwards and told her everything about a trauma filled Halloween from her childhood. It had something to do with a nightmare and a creepy doll. Can you believe it?"

The other kids just stared at her with their mouths hanging open.

"Well, at least we know Annie's mom doesn't like it either," said Steph. The kids laughed.

"We should get home. Let's meet up over here after lunch tomorrow if our parents let us, okay?" They all nodded in agreement. They left as Annie's mom was coming inside.

ANNIE WAS CHANGING INTO HER PAJAMAS FOR BED after her shower. What she overheard earlier in the day had left her heartbroken. She thought they were her friends, but maybe they weren't. She should have been sad about Brian, but she felt nothing at all.

Realizing that she'd left Clara in the living room after dinner, she went downstairs to get her. Thinking she heard something behind her, she turned around to look, but saw nothing. As she reached the last step, she stopped. What she saw was strange and sent chills down her spine. Goose pimples sprang up on her arms and she felt an icy breeze while the temperature dropped in the house. Her mom was standing in the kitchen staring into the living room, right at Clara. If Annie didn't know better, she would've thought Clara was staring right back. She shook her head to shake out the thoughts like earlier.

"Um, mom? I'm just gonna grab Clara and go to bed. Love you." Annie's expression went from curious to concerned when her mom didn't respond until she started walking up the stairs. She thought she saw the carpet appear to be foggy, but quickly dismissed it since she blinked and it was gone.

"Oh, what? My apologies, sweetheart. I completely spaced out, didn't I? I'm just tired. I'll be up in a minute to tuck you in." Kristi was not feeling well and exhaustion took over. Since her husband was out of town for work, she locked up the house and went upstairs to go to bed early. Before bed, she would usually tell Annie a story before she fell asleep, but she didn't feel like it tonight.

"Annie, what do you have planned for your last day of freedom tomorrow?" She laughed as she sat on the bed and tucked her in tight. Realizing her error in judgment, she backtracked.

"I'm so sorry, honey. I wasn't thinking."

"It's okay, mom. I might hang out with my friends again, I'm not sure. You know, I might just want to spend time with you, if you have time?"

"We can definitely hang out tomorrow. Eat all the ice

cream and snacks while we watch our favorite movies. You good with that?"

Annie nodded her head yes in agreement.

"Let's get some sleep tonight. I'm really sorry. I'm just not up for a story this time." Kristi kissed Annie on the forehead. "Love you bunches."

"Love you back more, mommy. It's fine. I'm sleepy too." Annie said in her sweet voice and closed her eyes.

She hadn't said "mommy" in a while, so that gave Kristi pause, and her heart melted. She turned around to shut the door quietly, and she was sure she saw the doll shift slightly in her daughter's arms. Kristi gasped out loud and covered her mouth in disbelief. *No. That didn't happen,* thought Kristi. She left the door ajar, just enough to let some of the hall light spill into Annie's dark room. She always insisted she had to have complete darkness and a fan on to sleep. Surprisingly, Annie didn't wake up when Kristi saw the doll move. Convincing herself that she saw nothing, she backed out of the room.

As she walked down the hall to her and Michael's room, she thought she heard faint carnival music. She didn't realize just how tired she really felt. She felt it in her soul and had to be hearing things. However, *sleep would be impossible now,* she thought. Changing into her t-shirt and sweatpants for bed, she noticed lightning in the distance. Her view of the lightning show was spectacular through her large bedroom window that overlooked the wooded area behind her house. *Of course, it would storm when Michael isn't here*, she thought.

She ran downstairs to grab a few small candles and a lighter from the junk drawer in the kitchen, then went back upstairs to her bedroom. She grabbed the Maglite she kept under her bed, which could double as a weapon. Not that she expected to need a weapon if the electricity went out. Thinking of Clara, she clutched it tightly. The solid weight of the cold metal felt reassuring in her hand. As she crawled into bed, her lids grew heavy and the strength to keep them open disappeared.

AS ANNIE AND KRISTI SLEPT, THE POWERFUL storm rolled in, loud and violent. The neighborhood lost power at 2:00 a.m. and Annie tossed and turned in a troubled sleep. About thirty minutes after the power went out, Annie got up to go to the bathroom. The hall light wasn't on, nor any of the other lights that her mom typically left burning when she retired for the night. When she came back, Clara wasn't where she'd left her, next to her pillow. She finally found her on the floor near the bed. She must have knocked her off it in her sleep. "Come here Clara," Annie muttered. She crawled back into bed with Clara and drifted quickly back to sleep. She didn't notice that Clara snuggled in, as a doll shouldn't be able to do. The lightning struck loudly as it lit up Annie's room. As Annie's mom stood in the hallway, checking on her daughter, in the brief flash of lightning, she saw a smile creep across Clara's face. The impossible image spiked fear through her heart, even as she was sure she was imagining it. Every hair on her body stood at attention as she slowly made her way to Annie. She gently woke Annie up to take her to her Grammy's house.

"Mommy, what is it? I'm so tired."

"Annie, the electricity is out and we need to go to Grammy Dawn's house for a while."

"Okay." Annie got up and grabbed Clara.

"Annie, you'll have to leave Clara here. It's raining outside, and she'll get ruined. You'll see her tomorrow."

"No! She has to go with us. She said she'd be lonely here by herself."

"Annie, seriously. She's expensive and she won't be worth much if she's ruined in the rain."

"She said she won't get ruined in the rain, mom, please!"

"Fine, let's go." Kristi grabbed Clara and tried to set her down on Annie's bed, but for some reason, she was stuck to her and she couldn't separate herself from the doll. Kristi stopped moving and just stared at nothing for what felt like an eternity.

Fog started rolling slowly and methodically inside from underneath the front door, quite like little cat feet, as the storm outside intensified. In just a few brief minutes, the fog was low and clung to every floor surface in the house.

Kristi whimpered like she was in pain, like someone does when they are shaken. Flashbacks assaulted Kristi's memory, but the memories were not her own. She saw a young woman who wore a beautiful and bright psychedelic top with flared sleeves, flared bell-bottom jeans, and white tennis shoes. Her long, flowing brown hair had a delicate floral headband holding her locks in place. She was headed to a Ferris wheel to run it and was attacked by another carnie. He knocked her to the ground, punched her in the face, and waited until she was passed out to do the unthinkable. Those memories faded and Kristi's spell was broken. She was herself again, albeit even more terrified.

Looking around and realizing that the fog was inside the house, Kristi snapped out of her disorientation.

"Mom, what are you doing? You're acting weird and I don't like it." Annie spoke with fear in her voice.

"Um, I don't really know. You know what? We don't

need to leave. I'm sure everything will be fine. I'll grab you a flashlight and a camping lantern that runs on batteries. It'll be like indoor camping. I'll be right back." She dropped the doll on the bed, gently.

"Stay in bed until this fog disappears. I'll be back soon."

Annie looked at her mom like she had lost her mind.

"Mom, it's not foggy in here. What are you talking about?"

"You don't see it? It's covering the entire floor!" Kristi was dumbfounded.

"No mom, there's nothing on the floor."

Sighing, Kristi relented, "Maybe I'm still dreaming, who knows? People can hallucinate when they are over-tired, right? I'll be right back."

"Oh, sure mom." Annie responded with exasperation.

Kristi headed back to her bedroom, grabbed the mini lantern from her closet, and went back to Annie's room. She set it down on the nightstand. "Here. Do you need me to wait until you fall asleep? I'll sit in your chair if you want?"

"I'm okay, mom. I just want to sleep."

"I'll check on you later then, okay?"

"Okay, Mom. I love you."

"I love you too."

Annie snuggled back in bed with Clara and was fast asleep in minutes.

KRISTI TRIED TO DO THE SAME, BUT SHE COULDN'T. Something was amiss, and she couldn't quite put her finger on what it was. *That fucking doll,* she thought. She lay in bed for what felt like forever, but when she checked the clock, it had only been twenty minutes. Sleep was a lost cause at this point. She kept thinking about the carnival assault memory that appeared out of nowhere. Believing it had something to do with Clara, she needed to figure out what was going on.

She quickly got dressed, went downstairs, then sat and tried to pull herself together while waiting for the coffee to cool enough to drink. Grabbing her cup, she moved to the living room to watch tv. Unable to concentrate on a show or even watch the news, she flipped through channel after channel, eventually turning off the television as they were reporting on Brian's death. She was trying to keep her fears at bay. Pretending normalcy wasn't working on calming her nerves. She dreaded going back upstairs to check on Annie. No parenting manual she'd read had prepared her for a doll that showed signs of life.

When she padded back upstairs and reached Annie's bedroom, she slowly pushed the door open as far as it would go. The lantern was off. Her night light didn't come back on either. The power was restored just before she made her coffee, so she was unsure of why the room was dark. The storm had passed, but heavy spitting rain remained, with reverberating sounds at Annie's window. What she saw next was every parent's worst nightmare. Annie was still fast asleep. Clara remained in bed next to Annie and was held tightly in her arms. Next to the doll stood a ghostly figure of a young woman, likely in her early twenties. She looked up and stared directly into Kristi's eyes with a soulless abyss of black holes where her eyes should be. They both stared at each other for a moment, then the ghost rushed at Kristi. It was like a hurricane force wind knocked into her, and she fell against the wall. She felt extremely disoriented and tired.

More memories; not her own, were running through her mind. She saw a young woman referred to as Sharon. Balled up in the fetal position, Sharon sobbed as only someone that had experienced true terror and the evils of the world could. The man that hurt Sharon returned with vengeance in his eyes.

"Sharon, you need to understand that there is an order

in which things run around here. If you go against that, you pay the price. You get it?"

"Because I refused to have casual sex with you? You think you can treat me any way you want, because you are a man in charge? Did I get that right?"

"Funny bitch, aren't you?"

"No, Dan, just leave me alone. I'll leave the group. Right now, I'll leave!"

Dan encroached on Sharon's space quickly and yanked her up to a standing position. Spittle escaped his mouth as he sneered at her. "Listen here, you dumb bitch. Do as I say, or you won't see another fucking day!"

Sharon gained footing and pulled a knife out from behind her back and plunged it into Dan's throat. She pulled it out as she had intended to slice through the jugular and an uncontrollable amount of blood was spurting out. She had hit her mark. Dan collapsed to his knees, then fell face down on the ground. Blood continued to pool around him. Sharon had the knife held up nearly above her head and her blouse was turning crimson. A roadie saw what happened, pulled his handgun out of his waistband, and shot Sharon in the head. She fell over on top of Dan's body. Since he didn't see the full confrontation, Dan's avenger didn't know she was only protecting herself.

Kristi snapped out of the dreamy fog she was in with

a pounding headache, and sat for a moment. Confused, she looked around and was slow to rise. She finally headed to her room, using the walls as support. She had the urge to sleep, as if it was all she *could* do. A ghost using her body as a conduit was exhausting and had stolen every ounce of energy from her. Her mind turned as it attempted to process why this was happening. Feeling gratitude for eventually reaching her bed, she fell into it and fell asleep immediately. Dreams hijacked her mind while she slept. In her dream, Dawn, her own mother, was running from something and turned around with a look of disbelief.

"No, no, no, get away!" Kristi yelled and woke herself up.

After Kristi slept restlessly, she was driven to check on Annie again. She felt *off*. Grasping why she was having visions of someone else's life escaped her. Dreaming about her own mom was bizarre at best. She felt like something was inhabiting her, and her body was no longer her own. Quiet feminine whispers began chanting in her mind.

"Stop it! Go away! Leave me alone!" Kristi screamed as she dropped the flashlight she had unknowingly grabbed and clutched her head with both hands. She closed her eyes and sunk down to the carpet in the hallway. Fog had appeared again, surrounding Kristi. She could hear a feminine voice laughing at her. Sharon separated herself from Kristi and spoke to her, and Kristi's body slumped forward.

The ghostly figure of Sharon that Kristi saw spoke to her, but only in her thoughts. "*My name was Sharon. I belonged to a small traveling circus working as a carnie and running the rides in the 1970s. No one cared when I was gone. I cared. I vowed I would walk the earth until I found the man that murdered me, but he is likely dead too. Taking up residence in a doll isn't ideal, but now I can inhabit you instead, and I'll have my revenge. You can't stop me!*" Laughter could be heard in every crevice of their home.

Sharon's image dissipated into thin air. Kristi began shaking uncontrollably and then passed out. Minutes later, Kristi regained consciousness. Holding her Maglite, she went towards Annie's room. She saw that Annie wasn't there, but the doll's red hair was fanned out on the pillows. She lifted the heavy steel Maglite above her head and she struck the doll's head with the force of a mother's fear. She lost control of herself while repeatedly bringing the flashlight above her, then down, finally relenting solely due to exhaustion. Gasping for air, she felt her heart race in her chest. She had to find a trash bag in order to remove the doll before Annie caught sight of it. For Annie to see the doll smashed to pieces would be unthinkable and would scare her. She pulled back the covers to pick up the pieces and gasped at what she saw. She let out a guttural whimper, then screamed until her vocal chords were raw.

Under the pink bedspread and covers lay sweet Annie. Her beautiful face was unrecognizable and her brain matter covered the soft pink pillow cases in red. Kristi didn't understand how that could happen; she fell to the floor in heartbreak, anger, and confusion. Moments later the doll reappeared on the bed. Separating herself from Kristi again, Sharon's image spoke. *"I told you that you couldn't stop me."*

Kristi looked up when she heard the phone ring, but stayed where she was in Annie's bedroom. She couldn't bring herself to move, and felt compelled to be with what remained of her daughter. Sharon was hovering in the dark corner of the bedroom. Kristi had no idea what time it was or even what day. She heard something downstairs and her ears perked up and listened like an animal in the wild.

"Kristi, honey, I'm home. Annie, daddy's home. The kids outside want to hang out."

Kristi looked over at Sharon, just as she slowly disintegrated into nothing. The image rippled as though wind whispered through it, fading out slowly. *Nooooooo, not him too,* she thought. She panicked, began weeping again, and heard heavy footsteps come up the stairs. Michael stopped at the doorway to Annie's room. He saw what remained of his daughter in her bed, and his wife on the floor next to her with a wild and crazed expression, and he realized she had lost all of what little sanity she'd had left. He nearly collapsed in grief and was completely devastated. Tears streamed down his face, and he sobbed like he had never had in his life. Sharon was behind him.

"Why Kristi, why? Why would you do this to our baby? Our only baby! She was beautiful and perfect! *Why, Kristi*?"

He screamed at the top of his lungs in despair and obvious anger. Sharon thrived on heightened human emotions and used this opportunity to slip inside Michael. He shifted and slightly shook like he was adjusting to a new body.

Is that what I looked like when she did that to me? Kristi wondered.

Michael moved toward her, and she thought for a fleeting moment that all was forgiven. Rushing forward, he aggressively seized her by the ankles, pulling her down on her back. He crawled on top of her. He gripped her head like a vice and slammed it down multiple times on the carpet. Kristi's skull cracked.

Sharon slipped out of Michael and floated in the

space above Kristi. She also had fiery hair, and beautiful, translucent skin. Michael was mesmerized, then looked terrified and confused all at once. Not understanding what had happened, he looked all around at the carnage that lay before him. He still straddled Kristi, and he whimpered, moved away from her, and cowered in the corner across from Sharon. The ghostly figure that looked like Annie's doll never took her vacant eyes off of him. He began uncontrollably sobbing and continued to cower in the corner for some time until there was banging at the front door.

"Kristi, it's mom. Are you guys home?"

Sharon looked at Michael and put a finger to her lips and whispered, "Shhhh." She disappeared into a dark crevice of Annie's room, waiting.

Dawn could be heard coming upstairs. Not finding Kristi in her own room, she moved along to Annie's bedroom doorway. When she peeked into her granddaughter's room, she thought her mind was playing tricks on her. So much was wrong with this picture. Feelings of anxiety, grief, and disbelief bubbled to the surface as her heartbeat quickened. She screamed.

"Dawn, it's so groovy to see you again. Remember me?" Sharon's ghost snickered.

Dawn looked at Michael, pleading with her eyes and not understanding any of this.

"Who are you? What's happening here?" Dawn spoke with a whisper. "Michael?"

Michael looked at his mother-in-law, where she saw the fear in his eyes that mirrored her own. She knew he wasn't responsible for the carnage that lay before her.

She remembered running for her life during the carnival of 1973.

"Dawn, I know you remember me. How could you possibly forget? Funny how you thought you would never see me again. You left me in a *fucking doll*. Do you know how long I was in that doll before I could get out?"

"Oh, no. Sharon, I'm so sorry about what happened to you, but I had nothing to do with it!"

"Really? You didn't tell Mick to shoot me because you were in love with Dan and you wanted me out of the way?"

"That was so long ago, and we were all so young. I didn't ask him to do that. I'm not a murderer. "

"It doesn't matter, anyway. You could grow old and have a family. *My* life was cut short. Patiently, I have waited for you for decades and I can't tell you how happy I am to see your family die, but most enjoyable of all, will be seeing *you* die."

"Sharon, just stop. It's not going to bring you back! You murdered my family, isn't that enough?" Sobbing, Dawn dropped to her knees in the doorway of Annie's room. She noticed fog appear out of nowhere and faint carnival music began playing from some unknown location.

"Dawn, it'll never be enough. I enjoy being caught between the living and the dead, and I prefer the dead. It's less complicated when you no longer have to deal with someone. Don't you agree?"

Sharon moved over to Michael and entered his body swiftly. He acclimated more quickly than last time. Michael rose from the floor and gave Dawn an unobstructed view of her grown daughter. His wicked grin grew wide and sinister as he cautiously crept toward her. Dawn struggled with what she was seeing on the floor. Kristi's head was no longer identifiable and in pieces. Blood was everywhere and had seeped into the carpet, turning it deep red in some places and pink in others.

"Dawn, come here. I have a surprise for you!" Michael called out to Dawn.

THE FOG IN THE HOUSE WAS THICK, AND DAWN used it to her advantage to try to get away. The carnival music volume increased as she padded down the stairs as quietly as she could. She ran for the front door faster than she thought possible.

"Come out, come out wherever you are!" Michael yelled.

Dawn didn't stop running until she smashed into the front door. Even with momentum born of desperation and fear, the door wouldn't budge when she tried to swing it open. As hard as she yanked, pushed, pulled, kicked, and wrenched at the door, it wouldn't move; maybe this was where the evil would take its final victory. She looked over her shoulder as she continued to try to open the door. The fog was thick, and the music was loud. It was distracting Dawn from thinking of an alternative way of getting out.

Michael's image once more sprang from the mist, but it was Sharon's voice that came from his mouth. "Oh mother, there you *are*! I've been trying to find you. Don't leave, we haven't played yet. We can have so much fun together. Like the fun I had with Annie and Kristi!"

"Get away from me!"

"Now Dawn, what do you possibly have to live for now? I killed your family. Well, most of them anyway. Michael here doesn't count since he is your son in-law. I'm not sure what I'll do with him. Maybe I'll keep him?" Michael laughed.

He grabbed Dawn by the hair and pulled her back upstairs. She fought and struggled to free herself.

"Stop fighting me, bitch!" He punched her in the mouth multiple times.

Dawn mumbled something, but her mouth was swollen, filling with blood and she spit out a tooth as Michael continued to drag her to the stairs. She accidentally urinated as he shoved her down and kicked her in the side. Whimpering, she curled up in the fetal position. She knew in her mind that it wasn't really Michael doing this, but it was still difficult to not hate him, she thought.

While Dawn was nearly unconscious, Michael dragged her upstairs by her feet. Slowly pulling her up the stairs as her head bounced off the steps, he finally got her to the top of the stairs. Taking a break, he breathed deeply, resting for a moment. Sharon worked her way out of Michael's body. He collapsed on the stairs next to Dawn. He gazed over at Dawn and realized that she was barely breathing. The smell of blood and urine combined filled his nostrils, and he turned to the side and retched.

Sharon appeared in front of Michael and Dawn. "Your work is not finished yet, asshole."

"Please leave. You have ruined my family, my life. I know nothing about you. Take your damn doll and get the fuck out of here."

"That's not happening and you know it. I have to finish Dawn off."

Michael reached into his pocket and pulled out his rosary. He held it up towards Sharon and was praying.

"You idiot, I'm not a demon. I'm a fucking ghost. Crosses and shit don't affect me."

Dawn started coughing and caught the attention of the others. Sharon used this opportunity to use Dawn's body, hoping to end her. Dawn gripped the wall as she eased upward and tried to stabilize herself. She screamed and ran into the wall in the hallway. She backed up and ran her head into the wall again.

"Stop it, Stop! Please!" Michael pleaded with the ghost, but his words fell empty and meant nothing to Sharon. He went to Annie's room to grab the doll. He threw her against the wall, Clara appeared untouched except for blood trickling down her porcelain face.

Loud knocks could be heard over the dying carnival music, and the fog was dissipating. Dawn was still running herself into the wall, damaging the drywall with blood smeared around it. Dawn finally collapsed after hitting herself against the wall one final time. Michael tried to help her while he was leaning over her. Sharon went back into Clara but tracked Michael with the glassy green eyes.

"Police, open up!"

Michael cringed inwardly because he knew what this must look like.

"Upstairs, help! Please!" Michael yelled. He began to do chest compressions on Dawn, hoping to save her life.

The officers opened the door, took a moment to scan the area, and quickly went up the stairs.

"Sir, back away from her, now!"

Michael did as they asked. "I was trying to save her life. My family was dead when I got here!"

"Sir, put your hands behind your back." Michael did as he was told. The officer cuffed him and led him outside to the police vehicles. Michael was secured in the back of one of the SUVs. The paramedics arrived shortly after Michael was placed in the car.

The police and paramedics were now upstairs, and two officers peered into Annie's room.

"Holy fuck man, you see this shit?" "Yeah, what monster would do this?"

"He's secure in my vehicle," the third officer said.

Just at that moment, the three of them heard something and drew their guns simultaneously. They glanced around, but didn't see anyone. The only thing they saw was a creepy, bloody doll, with a twisted grin. The cops looked at each other and shuddered. They cautiously moved around the crime scene as the investigators joined them for a briefing, then took over in Annie's room.

The paramedics had Dawn on a stretcher with oxygen and hurried her to the ambulance so they could take her to the hospital. She was in terrible condition. Michael was on his way to the police station for questioning. The crime scene would take hours to process and then clean up. They worked well into the night. The last person who finally left the home locked the front door and made sure it was secure. Murder scenes can draw additional criminal activity, so the house would probably need a security guard until the case faded away from the town's memory.

As the lead detective was getting into her car, she thought she saw the upstairs curtains flutter and heard faint carnival music playing eerily in the distance. She felt an icy chill as she entered her car. She promptly locked the doors. Looking in her rearview mirror as she left, she saw a shadowy figure in Annie's window. Although Michael had sworn he was innocent during the interview and questioning, she was sure that he would be found guilty. With what she just witnessed though, Detective Larkin wasn't convinced of his guilt, but she would never admit to what she just saw. Silence will eat away at her forever while Michael suffered in prison for eternity.

PART TWO
FALL

HALLOWEEN MAYHEM
A SLEEPY HOLLOW STORY

Falling from her hands, she watched the knife hit the blood-spattered leaves in the woods behind his home. The chill in the air caused her to shiver and pull her black coat collar up closer to her ears. Releasing a sigh of relief, she was grateful for it all to be over. She will have been long gone by the time someone discovers his body. Bending over, she covered Lucas with leaves, branches, and dirt with her lined, gloved hands. No longer able to see the body, Madison was satisfied and walked away with all the confidence in the world that again, she would get away with murder.

TWO MONTHS LATER...

End of October included a few things; Halloween is near, winter is on the way, and the celebration season is about to commence. Moving to a new state and new small town meant Madison would have to be extra cautious to not let anything from her past leak out. Her new teaching position was a coveted one, as not many positions became available in Sleepy Hollow. She would have to be ready to field questions about why she was still single at thirty and why she moved. It's almost as if it's a crime to be attractive and unattached. People often confuse her confidence with conceit. Those she meets, just need to get to know her, then they'll see for themselves.

Her long dark brown hair, green eyes, porcelain skin, and fit figure, are off putting to some women. She knows that once they got to know her, they would love her. Her hopes were high that all good things and friendships were about to happen in this quaint small town that she's looking forward to exploring and settling down in.

As luck would have it, a cute cottage style home was for sale just on the outskirts of town across from the cemetery where Washington Irving was buried. Buying the home promptly after being hired to teach English at Sleepy Hollow High School for the literature position was almost too good to be true, and felt like a whirlwind. Madison Johnson did not live her life with regrets and decided rather quickly to pull the trigger on the purchase.

The front yard view from across the street with the small cemetery adjacent to the Old Dutch Church provides a haunting yet beautiful view. Trees lined the street with bright crisp orange and red leaves. Varied sizes of headstones and monuments were sprinkled throughout the cemetery, with several famous deceased buried in the historic Sleepy Hollow cemetery, drawing tourists throughout the year. Guided tours are conducted daily, so plenty of people are always watching. Evening tours are two hours, so she has to draw the curtains when darkness settles.

The first few nights, she's up past her bedtime, alternating playing on her phone, watching TV, and looking outside expecting to see things move in the night long after everyone else was inside. Daydreaming as she stared out at the cemetery and beyond created sinister images and crafted ideas for future creative projects. Her imagination provides endless fuel for her twisted mind. Often after midnight, she swears she hears heavy hooves hitting the pavement outside on the road in front of her house. Constant click-clacks of horseshoes for what seems like an eternity. Maybe this only happens in October. When she looks outside to see what is likely a horse, the streets are always dark and empty with no evidence of life outside.

GAZING OUT THE LIVING ROOM WINDOW AS SHE sips her black coffee, she thinks about all the things she needs to do, lest she forget about Lucas. Nothing has been reported about him missing yet, so she was growing more confident by the day that she, in fact, got away with it.

Madison stood up, grabbed her mug and went to the kitchen to make another cup of coffee. She loved to smell the freshly brewed coffee as the sun rose above the trees outside in the morning. Closing her eyes and breathing deeply for a moment before that first sip is always the best. Stretching out on the couch, setting her coffee down, she knows she needs to get motivated, but decides to read for a bit and rest first. Madison settles in with a good book, her comfy Burberry blanket, and her black coffee in hand. In her opinion, this is what a perfect late Saturday morning should look like.

Dozing off for a couple of hours was unexpected. Madison awoke with a start. She checked the time on her cell phone, and it was noon already. Guessing she needed the sleep, she wasn't going to worry about it all that much. She decided to unpack her life and get settled. Feeling comfortable is important, and especially *needed*, as the month would likely become more hectic as it inches closer to Halloween. Monday, she starts her new position. It's an unusual time in the school year to begin a new teaching position, but the other teacher disappeared, never to be heard from again, allegedly. She chuckled as she thought about that. That teacher was one disappearance she *didn't* have anything to do with.

After unpacking the kitchen in its entirety, Madison feels as though she accomplished a significant portion of the unpacking. She stacked the empty boxes in the garage, next to her car. She had finished unpacking her bedroom and the two bathrooms the day before. What she had left was most of her living area and her office, which was the other spare bedroom. Looking at the clock, she realized that it was approaching dinner time. She thought she would go for a walk before cooking. She grabbed a sweatshirt to pull over her t-shirt and dons her new tennis shoes.

WALKING BRISKLY DOWN THE STREET AND GAZING at the tourist activity, got Madison thinking about how active and run over with tourists this area will be soon. This street really is quite beautiful with the fall-colored leaves on all the trees lining both sides of the street. The trees arched over, nearly touching each other from either side. Beyond the historic cemetery is a small bridge that links the neighborhoods to the rest of the town. She decided to walk into town for dinner. She had her debit card and driver's license with her, so she relaxed as she contemplated where to go for dinner. Halfway across the bridge, she hears hooves galloping. What began as a whisper quickly turns into an inaudible yell. Running towards town across the bridge, Madison looked back. In the shadows of the trees beyond the bridge, she makes out shadows of what appears to be a horse and a rider.

The horse bucs, whinnies, turns, and rides away into the darkness.

Her heart races while she tries to calm herself internally. Her outward appearance to others is still that of confidence while she struggles with what the hell just happened.

Is that normal around here? She questioned herself.

WALKING INSIDE A HALLOWEEN THEMED PUB, SHE finds an empty bar stool and hops on. Looking around at her surroundings, she enjoyed the dark Halloween theme. Lights strung around the ceiling; lit Jack-o-lanterns carefully placed in the window ledges with lit candles on every tabletop. Haunting instrumental music plays in the background and mingles with the conversations throughout the pub. The bartender, a handsome man dressed in black, is prompt with her beer. They chat for a minute before a couple draws his attention away. When she finishes her beer, she plans on holding his attention a bit longer the next time. Unfortunately for him, she's made him her evening goal and end game. No ring graced his ring finger, so she has high hopes. Truth be told, it isn't necessarily a deal breaker.

Trying to see if he had a name tag so she could get his attention quicker, she sees that his name is Tom.

"Tom? Hi, over here."

Madison calls to him and smiles, attempting to gain and keep his attention on her and only her, for as long as possible.

"Yes, can I help you?" Tom asks.

"Of course you can. I'd like a dirty Stoli martini, shaken, not stirred, up, with extra olives. Yes?" Madison asks, mustering the most innocent, yet seductive expression she can.

"I can make that for you…what's your name?"

"Madison, but you can call me Madi if you want." Flirting with Tom seems to be working.

"Madi, how's this?" He set her drink in front of her.

"Mmm. Delicious. Thank you. You've been working here for a long time? I just moved here so I need all the inside info on all things Sleepy Hollow, Tom."

"I've been here for about a year. I only work weekends because I'm a teacher at the high school. I teach history."

"Well Tom, that's interesting! I just accepted the new English department opening and start Monday. Small world."

She puts her hand on top of his briefly, but not for long. She doesn't want to appear creepy. Withdrawing her hand, she begins to talk about her move here and where she lives.

"So, tell me about living here." Madison asks Tom.

"It's a fun little town to live in. There are some things you gotta watch out for though. Growing up here, we are told these things, and it's mainly tourists and new people to the area that fall victim if you will. Considering where you said your home is located, and you walked, I'm guessing that you know what I'm talking about, right?" Tom was washing glasses as he waited for a response, looking at Madison with his chocolate brown eyes.

"I'm not sure what you mean. Are you referring to the horse and the rider that went after me? Madison inquires, looking deep into his eyes and trying to keep him interested.

"Well, that's blunt." He replies, laughing. "But yeah, that's what I mean. Not everyone has been so lucky. You wonder why there's a job opening for the position you just accepted? Jacob disappeared and there is no explanation other than that." Tom states with assurance.

Madison smiled to herself, knowing that there were other pliable reasons he could've disappeared, but leaves it alone.

"Long story short, don't cross the bridge alone?" Madison asks.

"Well, that and definitely not on Halloween." Tom warns.

Tom goes to tend to other customers while Madison ponders his parting words. Not really understanding what that means, she supposed that she would find out soon enough. She leaves more than enough money to cover the two drinks and decides to go somewhere else for dinner. She leaves her name and number on a sheet of paper with the cash, in case he's interested in talking to her more. She imagines that she will see him within a couple of days.

Walking around the quaint small town, she sees a small Italian restaurant and decides to duck in for dinner. Seated in the bar area with a window view, she gazes out at the town that has become her home, hopefully for the long haul. She orders a coffee, manicotti, and a Greek salad. Sipping on her water, she thinks about what she needs to do at home before Monday, as well as what she can do to make Tom hers. Speak of the devil, an unknown number of texts.

I know what you did to Lucas.

That wasn't Tom. Who the fuck is that? Madison wonders. She blocks the number and forgets about it as her food arrives, along with her black coffee with cream.

Dinner is the best she's had had in such a long time. She knows that this place will become a regular spot for her. After paying, she gets a coffee to go and decides that she'll walk back to the pub that Tom was at. She wants to see if Tom can give her a ride home. She wants to get there safely without worrying about whatever *that thing* was that momentarily chased her. Looking around, there seemed to be bustling activity throughout the small town. Halloween was Monday, so that's wasn't surprising. The small town was so picturesque, and she loves it already.

WALKING INTO THE PUB THE SECOND TIME, TOM looks up at her and smiles so big, his cheeks must hurt. She grabs a bar stool close to him.

"Hi again." Madison says, with kindness and hope.

"Hi Madi."

"What time are you off work tonight?" Madison asks, hoping it's soon.

Looking at his watch, Tom sees it's shortly after 8:00 p.m.

"I should be done at 9:00 p.m., why?" He queries innocently.

"Well, I was hoping for a nightcap and a ride home?" Madison looks at him with her big green eyes and bats them in eager anticipation.

"I can do that. I have to clean up and tab everyone out, then I'll join you. Cool?" Tom checks.

"That works for me. I'll have one of those amazing martinis while I wait." Madison smirks and gives Tom her sexiest smile.

Madison sips her drink while she plays on her phone and watches Tom work. Even though they've just met, she can't help imagining what life would be like with him. Thick, dark, tousled hair that falls slightly over his eyes; deep brown almond shaped eyes that could bore holes in your heart, olive skin and a smile that won't quit. He's got a nice build and stands a couple inches over 6 feet. Tom has a fun personality too, and appears to be single. Seeing him every night and every morning would be a dream come true, until it wasn't anymore. She often grows tired of the same man, but for now, she wants to have a little fun.

Continuing to daydream, which she often does, she gazes out the pub windows. As the night draws on, the activity outside begins to slow. It seems that this town shuts down around now, and would likely be a ghost town by the time she and Tom leave. Less distractions are best to gain the attention she needs from Tom anyways.

Something out of the corner of her eye catches her immediate attention from outside, drawing her to the creepy bridge and beyond to the trees. She can't tell what it is, but something lurks in the shadows, and she shivers. It remains stationary as if it's waiting for something or someone. She definitely sees something out there, as this is not a figment of her imagination. Grabbing Tom's arm and his attention, she points toward the shadows in the woods.

"Tom, do you see that?" Madison's voice goes up an octave, as she's beginning to get a little nervous.

"What? See what?" Toms asks, confusedly.

"Outside in the woods!" Madison hollers excitedly.

"No, I don't see anything. What do you think you saw?' Tom asks.

"I—I don't know." She mutters.

Beyond the trees nothing can be seen any longer and Madison is stumped. She knows that she can have an overactive imagination, but she's confident that there is something out there. Something nefarious remains, she is sure of it.

PULLING INTO MADISON'S DRIVEWAY, TOM IS wearing an expression that shows an internal struggle, as Madison looks at him with smoldering eyes, she hopes that her sexuality is wielding great indestructible power over Tom.

"Would you like to come in for a drink? I can pour you a whisky if you'd like?" Madison invites.

"Well, that depends, what kind of whisky do you have? Because if it's shitty, the answer will be no." He has a goofy grin on his face, which is irresistible.

"I have my favorite, Old Forester. It's an oldie, but definitely one of the better whiskeys." Madison touts.

Tom turns off the car. "What are you waiting for? Pour me that whiskey." Laughing, Tom gets out of the car and opens the car door for Madison.

"Ok, then." Madison says joyfully.

Smiling and enjoying the banter, she got out and went promptly to the front door to let Tom in. He follows her in, and shuts the door. Madison puts her house keys, driver's license, and debit card in a bowl on the entryway table. Moving to the kitchen, she grabs two highball glasses and adds a couple of cubes of ice to each of them. She pours generously into both glasses.

"Cheers to a new town, job, and blossoming friendship." Madison states as she clinks her glass against Tom's.

They sip their drinks quietly for a moment.

"You hungry? I can put in a frozen pizza or make sandwiches?" Madison asks.

"Madi, that's sweet. I'll take a sandwich, I'm starving. I'm not picky at all. I appreciate it." Tom answers.

After their sandwiches, whiskey, and conversation has run its course for the evening, Tom gets up to leave.

"Madi, thanks for everything. I'm exhausted, but it was great to meet you. I'll see you at work Monday and I'm looking forward to work now more than ever. I'll give you the grand tour and everything before school starts. Here is my cell number if you need anything." Tom hands her a Post It note with his name and number on it.

"Thank you so much. I had a great time tonight and I look forward to Monday. Can you meet me in the parking lot so we can walk in together?"

"Of course. Just text me when you get there, and we'll meet by the back door on the east side of the building. Sound good?" Tom asks.

"Yes, of course. Thank you for welcoming me to your beautiful town" Madison says softly.

"It's beautiful, but it can be scary too. Just don't go out at night alone." Tom kisses Madison on the cheek and lets himself out.

Well, what the fuck does that mean? Madison wonders out loud to no one.

Madison is too wired to go to bed yet. She pours herself another whiskey, sits on the couch, and cracks open the book she's been reading. It was some smut book her friends Laura and Caroline recommended. She's never read a book like this before and while it is written well, she knows it just isn't her "thing". Give her murder and mayhem all day every day. While she is sipping her last whiskey and reading the last few chapters in her book, she thinks she hears a horse outside. She looks out the window, but doesn't see anything. Deciding to get up and stretch her legs, she sauntered over to the front door and opened it. She steps out onto the small porch area and looks all around outside. Darkness has enveloped the town since nightfall, which was hours ago.

Across the street in the cemetery was a sleek black horse with a rider cloaked in darkness. The horse whinnies and is stomping in agitation. Suddenly it broke and is galloping right toward her! She stands there frozen, in complete shock; sinister laughter can be heard which brings her out of her hypnotic fear. She quickly turns and runs back inside, slamming the door behind her. Galloping can be heard trailing off into the distance. Her heart races. She knows that was real, no doubt about it. She thinks about calling Tom, but knows he's tired, and she'd feel bad disturbing his probable slumber.

Sleep seems a distant possibility, but she knows she

has to try. Madison locks up all the doors and windows, shuts the lights off, and walks back to her bedroom in hopes of passing out and sleeping like a queen. She changes into comfortable sweats and a t-shirt for bed, beginning to unwind and relax a bit. Crawling into bed and running the day back through her mind, she tries to figure out what to do tomorrow, helping calm her so she can sleep. She snuggles up with the fan on and the covers pulled up to her chin. She closes her eyes and drifts into a sleep that is broken, but still, she manages to get some rest.

Yawning and slowly opening her eyes, she peers down at her phone to check the time. She doesn't have anywhere to be and isn't concerned with the fact that she's slept in until 9:00 am. She sees a text from someone she doesn't know. She opens it and reads:

Meet me at the cemetery today at 4:30 pm

Who is this?

You'll see at 4:30

Madison hates surprises. She likes to have most everything in her life planned out. She feels more accomplished and productive that way. For a surprise meeting, having no idea who they are, is completely unnerving. She decides that at 4:00 p.m. she'll start watching for someone across the street that stood out from the tours today. In the meantime, she decides she'll get out of the house and check out the neighborhood. Later she'd drive into town for lunch and make sure she is back here in time for whatever this "meeting is about.

Grabbing coffee and a banana, she sits on her comfy spot on her couch, leisurely sipping her coffee and eating her breakfast. She looks at her socials on her cell phone, chats with a few friends, then puts her phone down, and exchanges it for the TV remote. She clicks on the TV and looks for something interesting to watch. Settling for local news, there's an update on the teacher that's missing. She turns up the volume.

"Today in Sleepy Hollow, there is a new investigation underway. Taylor Cannon, the local high school teacher that went missing, his body has been uncovered and found in the woods. This missing person case has now turned into a homicide investigation. Cannon, thirty years old, had been teaching English at the high school for five years before he went missing. Foul play is suspected as his head was missing. More on the 10:00 o'clock news."

Interesting. A smile playfully hints at the corner of her mouth as she thinks about how there was another killer in the area besides her. Clicking off the television, she sits for a moment and finishes her coffee. Getting up from the couch, she picks up her mug and banana peel to deposit in the trash and puts the mug in the dishwasher. She peeks outside through the window that faces the street and the edge of the cemetery above her kitchen sink. Tours must be kicking in, since she sees all the people milling about. One person lingers toward the back from the crowds in the shadows near the edge of the cemetery and stares directly at her home. The figure is stationary and alone. Second thoughts of a walk are creeping into her mind and she's now determined to change her plans. Trees are dancing, the branches waving in the wind, and leaves are blowing down the street this morning, which also creates doubt of her plans. Now she's using any excuse she can to avoid going outside. She continues to stare out her window and looks down for a moment to scratch her knee. She returns her gaze to what was beyond her window, but the figure is gone. That's weird, she thinks.

Deciding to stick to the self-induced schedule, she changes clothes after breakfast and is ready for her walk around the neighborhood. It's creeping up on 11:30 am, leaving plenty of time to get in some exercise before lunch. For safety, she grabs her purple pocket knife she keeps in her bedroom nightstand. She shoves it in her black crossbody bag with her car keys, cell phone, driver's license, debit card, gum, and lipstick. She still plans on going to lunch after her quick walk. Putting the bag over herself and adding a jacket, she secures her bun with a mist of hairspray, then walks from her bedroom to the front door and locks it behind her.

TURNING LEFT, SHE WANTS TO CHECK OUT PART OF the street she hasn't been able to explore yet. All the cottage style homes are so quaint and beautiful. Everyone's yards are well manicured, and fall flowers and jack-o-lanterns don most porches on either side of the street, just proving how wonderful this town is. Halloween decorations just upped the cool factor because most homes are decorated with lights, yard inflatables, and "larger than life" fake spiders and mummies. Madison begins to relax as she continues her walk down the street. Her street comes to an abrupt end with woods in front of her, as she looks at the last decorated home to her left. As she turns to head back to her home, she hears the rustling of leaves from the woods. Whispers soon follow with an increase of leaves and twigs breaking. Madison breaks in a full speed run toward her home. When she turns to look back, she trips on a crack in the pavement and falls. She looks toward the wooded area again and doesn't see or hear anything.

"Damn it to hell!" Madison curses. Anger begins to bubble to the surface, but she needs to keep it in check. The last thing she needs is for someone to see her lose her shit. Brushing off her knees, she then uses her palms to get back up. She stands there for a moment and looks around to ensure no one is watching her. She doesn't see anyone, but has a bad feeling regardless. Closing in on her home, she's relieved to get in the garage and jump into the car. She starts her car, backs out, and shuts her garage. Looking in the rearview mirror she thinks she saw someone hiding behind a headstone in the cemetery. Double checking her side mirror, there's something or someone cowering next to a large, crumbling headstone. Most details are obscured, but the form is large, even as it's bent over trying to hide in the shadows of the trees and behind the headstone itself. Shivering, she doesn't dismiss it, but decides to focus on getting out of there as quickly as she can.

DRIVING OVER THE WOODEN BRIDGE THAT WAS largely eventful last night, proves to be more desolate and less exciting now. Finding a place to park in town is no easy task, but Madison finally is able to finagle her way in quickly to a spot after someone just pulled out. Briskly walking to the pub where she met Tom; lunch there sounds like her best idea so far today. As she approaches the door, she glances up at the nearby bridge and notices the same figure watching her from earlier. Now she knows that she is being followed by someone.

Choosing to sit at the bar again, she waits for the bartender to serve her. Unfortunately, it isn't Tom. A nice older gentleman named Bob fixes her a whiskey neat, and she orders a Rueben sandwich with steak fries that was raved about by bar patrons the night before. She just needs to eat something. She isn't hungry, but knows her body needs the fuel. The bartender is polite and efficient, so that's all she cares about at this point.

When the food arrives, she's on her second whiskey, and is famished. The sandwich is great, and the fries are perfect, in spite of her earlier lack of appetite. It's a shame that she can't eat like this all the time. After lunch, she pays and gets up to leave. Tom is coming in as she's leaving. Her timing couldn't be worse. Sighing, she manages a smile for Tom.

"Hi Tom, I'm sorry I almost missed you. I popped in

for lunch before I had to go home to unpacking boxes and more work prep to get to."

"You know what to prepare already for your classes?" Tom asks in surprise.

Laughing, she responds with confidence, "Yes, I'll have the students work on a Transcendentalism unit first, then switch gears to something more fun. Do we do any cross-curricular planning or units?"

"Not really. We've talked about doing that. Maybe you can help this summer with curriculum mapping? We get free food from the pub." Tom throws in.

"Sure, I'd love to help. The food is great, so that sounds fun." Madison is fully invested in her conversation with Tom, not noticing that there's a storm brewing near Sleepy Hollow.

"See you in the morning? I seriously have unpacking to do, so 7:30 am?" Madison asked hopefully.

Tom responds with excitement, "Yes, definitely. I'll bring breakfast." He goes in for a hug and a quick peck on her cheek.

Madison's heart flutters. She can't help it. Walking back to her car, she looks around and notices the darkening clouds in the distance.

Great, she thinks to herself.

Going home and staying there for the night seems like the only option because she doesn't want to get stuck in the looming storm. She gets in her car and heads home across the bridge she's become wary of. Checking the time, she sees that it's closing in on 4:00 pm. Her secret meeting at the cemetery will be happening soon. As she pulls into the garage, she looks back toward the cemetery and doesn't see anything out of the ordinary there as the garage door closes and she goes inside her home.

She has some unpacking left to do in the living area so she starts with the wall of bookshelves. She coordinates by genre, last names, and color. Organization is important, and everything has its place, including people. Thinking about the fact that she still hasn't had an update on Lucas yet, but is interested in learning more about the teacher that went missing that she replaced. That case has piqued her interest. Her mind continues to wander as something catches her attention outside. She looks at her phone and sees a text that she missed.

See you soon. You look beautiful today.

Putting the phone back in her back pocket, she feels uneasy now. Even more so than before. She grabs her pocket knife and keys from her crossbody. She leaves through the front door and locks it behind her. Crossing the street to the cemetery, she remains in an open area. She knows people will be showing up soon for the tours, so she shouldn't be as worried as she feels. As she stares at her street before her, intently looking down both sides, the crunching of leaves and debris can be heard behind her. Quickly turning around, she sees someone stop just beyond the shadows of the trees. She can tell that it's a man, but the features are blurred by the shadows and she can't tell if she knows him or not.

"Madison, it's so nice to see you doing well," whispers the man in the shadows.

The storm approaches Sleepy Hollow more quickly than what the weather reports mentioned on the news. Rumbles of thunder are increasingly louder each passing moment and flashes of lightning brighten the cemetery and everything around it long enough to see who's stalking Madison.

"Lucas. I left you for dead. Why are you here? You should be...six feet under." Madison hisses.

"Luckily, someone found me shortly after you left me and I *did* nearly die. Fortunately for you, I didn't share that I knew who did this to me. I figure taking my own revenge on you will be sweet enough." Lucas cackles.

No one is showing up for tours, Madison noticed. Inclement weather must be an automatic cancellation or reschedule situation. This makes her as nervous as Lucas showing up unexpectedly did. She can't kill him again. Not here, that'll be suspicious. She backs up cautiously.

Even though it isn't late in the evening, darkness rolls in with the menacing clouds and it appears as if it'll stick around for a while. The sun isn't visible any longer, not even a sliver of light is available to give Madison hope of escaping. Lucas looks hungry and out for blood. He lunges at Madison and knocks her over. They hit the ground together, and roll around. He lands on top of her and has her arms pinned, immobilizing her. Punching her in the face twice and giving her a bloody nose, he slowed down her ability to fight. He stands up and kicks her in the side. Madison doubles over in pain and to protect herself.

In the distance she hears the all too familiar sound of hooves hitting the pavement and the whinnies of the horse. She can't even move to dash and hide in her house. Lucas begins looking around as he hears the same sounds as well as the sinister laughter that accompanies the horse moving swiftly toward them. Lucas stretches his neck and head to look around for what's coming, but it happens so fast, he doesn't have time to react.

The Headless Horseman wields a sword and quickly comes down on Lucas with a swift movement that severs his head. The ghostly Headless Horseman picks up Lucas' head from the ground, rears back on his horse, and lets out a booming sinister laugh and gallops away, leaving the corpse of Lucas and a terrified Madison. Hearing noises coming from the trees, she scrambles to get up as quickly as she can and slowly limps to her house. She hopes no one saw what happened, because that would be difficult to explain.

STARTING A NEW JOB WHILE NOT FEELING WELL IS not ideal after having the shit beat out of you. Thought Madison.

Being kicked and punched will require an ice pack, soaking in a hot bathtub, and Ibuprofen to hopefully offset the injuries and frankly, to not look rough. Considering how Lucas met his demise, again, she can't call the police or go to the hospital. Some unfortunate soul will happen across his remains. It just can't be her.

Madison starts her hot bath and gets her things ready for bed. She takes three Ibuprofens and chugs a glass of water. She had poured a glass of wine, but left it in the kitchen, on the counter. She heads back to the kitchen for her wine As she grabs it from the countertop, she looks out the window above her sink and sees something looking back at her. She screams.

She shot her glass of wine like a shot of whiskey and slammed it down, shattering the wine glass in the sink and cutting her thumb in the process. Grabbing a towel to stop the bleeding, she looks outside again, and notices something in the distance, near the trees by the cemetery. Whatever it is has left her alone for the time being.

What kind of place did I move to? Thinks Madison.

Putting a band-aid on her finger, she then makes sure all the shades are down and the doors and windows are locked this time. Normally she's the predator, but here, the tables have turned. She doesn't like it and things will need to change.

Sleep can't come fast enough. After she shuts her eyes, she drifts to sleep quickly.

When morning arrives , the alarm clock beeps, and Madison has to hit snooze a couple of times. Feeling incredibly sore from last night, she soon opens her eyes and realizes this is day one of the new job. Slowly rising, she's reluctant to start the day. The simple task of standing in front of her closet, trying to decide what to wear, proves difficult with the headache. Choosing khaki slacks, a black sweater with a Halloween scarf and silver jewelry, pairing them with black heels, she feels the look is good. Now she just has to style her hair and do her make up. After she's ready, she makes herself coffee and a protein shake for breakfast. She sits to watch the news and scrolls through her socials on her phone as she drinks the shake and sips her coffee. She feels that easing into the day is best and as luck would have it, she doesn't have to leave for work yet. One more cup of coffee and a few Ibuprofens will help with the pain and being tired, even though she thinks she got enough sleep.

HALLOWEEN EXCITEMENT IS EVERYWHERE. THE school is decorated in all things Halloween, from bales of hay and pumpkins, jack-o-lanterns, and lights. All the classroom doors were decorated because of a door decoration contest that the students and faculty vote on, as well as the public on their social media page. Before school is over, they will announce the winners. The prizes are a catered luncheon, a Barnes & Noble gift card, and a day off without using time off or writing sub plans. That's an amazing prize package and Madison thinks this town knows how to do Halloween right. If her door wins, that might not be fair since she's just starting here. They may not even include it actually, since the teacher is gone.

Madison waits by the doors for Tom. After just a few minutes of waiting, he arrives with coffee and breakfast burritos. Two of Madison's favorite things and Tom is becoming a close third.

Geez, am I becoming soft? Madison wonders.

"Thank you so much Tom, this is amazing. Coffee and breakfast burritos are my favorite."

"You're welcome, let's go to the faculty office to eat, students will bother us in the classroom." Tom says light-heartedly.

Watching Tom interact with colleagues and students, she can tell that he's well liked here. She has a great feeling about him. He introduces her to everyone they interact with until they reach a table to sit with each other and eat their breakfast. Madison is grateful all she had this morning was a protein shake, so she's a little bit hungry. The coffee and burritos are to die for.

Tom asked, "Are you excited for your new job? It's the best to start here on Halloween, so it should be a fun day. There's an assembly this afternoon so we have a modified schedule too."

"Yes! I'm sure today will be amazing. What happens tonight though? Trick-or-Treating? Parties? Halloween seems big here!"

"The kids Trick-or-Treat in town at all the businesses, then everyone eats at all the restaurants for dinner. After that, everyone does their own thing. Kids and their friend groups go to someone's house to trade candy and some have sleepovers. A few families host Halloween parties. It's a fun night."

"Sounds great. What will you do to celebrate tonight?" Madison asks.

"Oh, oh you know, the typical animal and human sacrificial thing." Tom quips.

"That sounds interesting. Do you take on any ghosts by chance?" Madison asked seriously.

"Madison, I'm kidding." Tom looks concerned.

"Oh I know, but I'm seriously asking, have you seen ghosts around here? There's strange things happening here."

"Um, look, we need to get to our classrooms, the bell is about to ring soon. Do you have your device yet?"

Madison patted her bag to show him she does indeed have her computer and everything she needs.

"Ok, good. Let me show you where your room is."

Tom squeezes her hand in an affectionate way, so that calms Madison down internally. The last thing she needs is to exhibit an angry outburst. She follows him to her new classroom, and they part ways.

She has the first period off for planning, so she doesn't have students filtering in her room yet. She opens her door and turns the light on in case any students want to come by and say hello. She makes her way over to her desk and sets up her laptop to start working. She doesn't have much to clean up, surprisingly. She takes down all the chairs for the students and looks through the cabinets for useful supplies. Afterwards, she sits at her desk to start mapping out the next few days. She taught AP juniors and on-level seniors. She loves this age group; they can be a lot of fun. Catching herself daydreaming, she cuts her eyes to the wall of windows in her classroom. The fall colors are beautiful. Watching the trees and the blue sky gives Madison hope that maybe things will work out. Behind one of the trees, something is amiss and watching Madison.

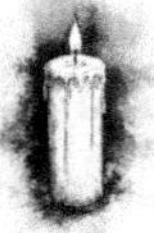

AFTER THE SCHOOL DAY IS OVER, TOM MAKES HIS way to Madison to see how her day went and if she agrees with the door winners. One of the art teachers won, as no surprise to Tom. They had a great conversation about their day at work and decided to catch happy hour at his pub.

"You sure you have time to join me for happy hour and maybe an early dinner?" Tom asks.

"I'd love nothing more." Madison happily agrees.

Madison follows Tom in her car to the pub, Horsemen Tavern, which is an unexpected surprise. She really likes Tom. Those intrusive thoughts that creep up every now and then have begun to bubble up, contained as a simmer, but those thoughts will result in action and boil over soon. She tries to have a relationship first in hopes of normalizing those feelings. Unfortunately, her taste for blood became palatable and the desire to repeat the atrocities that come easy to her are too strong to contain.

Tom arrives first and saves a seat for Madison at the bar. He orders appetizers and water to get them started. He looks forward to getting to know her better. He hopes that she'll be accepting of his true self. Sometimes people just couldn't get behind someone that might be a little unusual in extracurricular activities. He loves playing Dungeon and Dragons, and he hopes she would either enjoy it too or accept the fact that it was something he loves. He really enjoys her company, but isn't sure if she will want to date. He knows he's a bit nerdy.

Madison walks into the bar and sees Tom and moves to sit next to him. She ordered a whiskey neat and looked at his handsome face.

"So, what do you normally do for Halloween?" Madison asks Tom.

"Different things every year. I'm not one that traditionally does the same thing."

"Like what, though?" She laughs at his vague response.

"Oh, hanging out with friends usually. We will go out, or watch movies and play games like D&D. Have you heard of it?" Tom asks.

"Oh, yes. I had a boyfriend in high school that played that. He really enjoyed it. I thought creating the characters were fun, but I just don't have the patience for that type of game. I don't mind other people doing it. As long as I don't have to play." Laughing, Madison squeezes Tom's hand in assurance of acceptance.

"I was worried to tell you I have a nerdy obsession." Tom laughs.

"Well it's more innocent than mine, that's for sure. I'm obsessed with true crime. I find it fascinating." Madison is enthusiastic when she speaks.

Explaining the true crime obsession didn't give her secrets away. They enjoy the food and drinks, but are winding down after a couple of hours.

"Tom, you want to come over and hand out candy with me and watch a scary movie?"

"I'd love to. Let me clean up here and I'll join you at your home soon?"

"That works. I'll stop by the liquor store and you come by when you can."

Madison walks to the nearby liquor store to grab whiskey and wine, her two favorite alcoholic beverages. She deposits them in the backseat and drives the short distance home. Becoming leery of the bridge now, she double-checks that the car doors are locked every time she drives over it. Pulling into her garage she looks at the cemetery and notices yellow crime scene tape. She hadn't heard that they found the part of Lucas that remained after she ran off the night before. No one has questioned her yet, so that's a plus.

SHE PUTS THE WHISKY IN THE FRIDGE (SHE LIKES it cold) and the Cabernet on the counter, then she pulls out the glassware for each. She isn't sure which one Tom will prefer. She goes ahead and pours a whiskey and pads to the living room to get out the bowl of candy she threw together this morning. She tries to get good candy, not the crappy stuff she sees some people give out. She makes sure the porch light is on. She has no idea if anyone trick-or-treats in the neighborhoods since it seems most families here go to town and frequent the businesses instead. She's beginning to understand why. Here, the things that go bump in the night will kill you and maybe she was the last person to find out since she's new here. Madison has an idea what likely happened to the teacher she replaced, and she doesn't want to join him and what she can only assume are countless others.

A knock on the door startles Madison out of her thoughts. Rising from the couch, she grabs the bowl of candy and opens the door. No one was there. She steps out and looks up and down the street, the homes dark and everything is eerily quiet, and no kids can be seen. There's no way to tell if any of the residents were home. No porch lights were on, no cars were parked on the street, no children's laughter could be heard echoing from homes beyond hers. Madison is used to tons of families milling around eating and drinking, pulling boozy wagons to ease the chaos of the night with drinks to cope with the children high on sugar for hours. Desolation on Halloween night was certainly far scarier than any horror movie she had seen or real life horror she created herself.

Oh shit, this is weird. Thinks Madison.

Closing the front door, locking it, and shutting off the light makes her feel a tiny bit better. She expects that Tom would have shown up by now. Looking at her phone, she sees a text from him. He's running late. She responds and tells him to hurry up. She can't decide if she wants to love him or kill him. There's a lot at stake tonight to determine Tom's fate. She pours another whiskey and waits for Tom. The doorbell sounds again. Sighing, she goes back to the door. She opens it blindly and it's Tom, finally. Behind Tom, there's someone dressed up as a ghost, a sheet with eye holes and all. The ghost is still and silent. There's no trick-or-treat bag and no other children around, and what's worse is that Tom doesn't seem to notice.

Madison quickly pulls Tom inside and shuts the door.

"Tom! Did you not see what was beyond you?" Madison elevated her voice and her tone was worrisome.

Laughing, he asks "What are you talking about?"

Annoyed, "Unbelievable. There was a GHOST behind you!" Madison is getting even more exasperated than she probably should.

"It is Halloween, that's not *that* uncommon, Madison."

"It seems to be *Tom*. Did you see any other kids out? No, you didn't. Would you mind telling me what's going on here?"

Madison's hands are on her hips and she's staring intently at him, outwardly displaying her expectations of full details from Tom.

"I really don't know what you're talking about. I'm seldom ever on this street. I don't know what happens here." Tom was confused by what Madison said.

"There was a ghost behind you and you didn't see it, or feel that it was there? It's been hanging around here and I have a feeling that might be why there aren't kids out on this street."

Tom's mouth hangs open in surprise. He starts shaking his head.

"I don't believe in ghosts, Madison. I'm sorry if you think there is one, but there must be some other explanation. Let's just have a drink and pick a movie to watch, yeah?"

Pursing her lips, she nods her head in agreement and goes to the kitchen to pour the two whiskeys. This is her third, but who's counting. She sees out of the corner of her eye the ghost is still hanging around by the trees in her front yard. She's not really scared of it, but not knowing its intent, she's uncomfortable with it lurking in the darkness on Halloween. Maybe this is why the house was available for a pittance. She snorts and laughs at the absurdity of the direction everything has taken now. Sighing deeply, she takes the drinks to the living room and joins Tom on the couch. They choose to watch the movie Hostel and settle in to enjoy the movie. About an hour later, galloping could suddenly be heard in the distance. This puts Madison on alert and Tom joins her in curiosity. If nothing else, hearing hooves on the pavement, getting closer by the second, is disconcerting.

Madison rises from the couch and when she reaches the front door, she opens it wide and looks outside. She doesn't see the ghost anymore, but instead sees the horseman with a flaming jack-o-lantern in place of a head. Black as night and shiny as newly polished Mary Jane's, the stallion carries the abomination which rides atop it, closing in the distance between them.

Tom's phone rings. He looks at Madison. He was still sitting on the couch, and Madison was keyed in to every word as he answered. When he hangs up, Madison, forgetting about the door, walks over to Tom.

"Who was calling you so late?"

"Oh, my wife. She was wanting me to pick up a couple of things when I head back home."

"I'm sorry, what the fuck, Tom! You have a *wife*? I thought we were dating and not once did you even think that mentioning that you have a wife, oh, I don't know, was important!?!"

Madison yelling at Tom had escalated and in anger she went outside and paced in her front yard. Tom follows her out and apologizes profusely. Tom doesn't notice the horseman coming up behind him. The horse rears up on its hind legs and whinnies loudly. The horseman's sinister laughter echoes up and down the street. Tom turns around and screams.

The horseman gallops past Tom, taking his head with him, severed clean. The horseman takes off his flaming jack-o-lantern, throws it at Madison who dodges it, and sticks Tom's head atop his neck. Cackling wildly, he stares at Madison.

Madison was livid. "He was *my* kill, you asshole!"

She threw the flaming jack-o-lantern back at him as he rode away in the darkness and disappeared across the wooden bridge. She turns and sees several ghosts in the graveyard. watching her from a safe distance. She looks down and sees the remainder of Tom's body in her yard.

Well, I guess his wife won't be getting those things from the store, she muses. Guessing she needs a tarp to wrap him up in so she can dump the body, she goes inside to see if she has one or two. She quickly runs to the door and darts inside. When she reaches her kitchen, she pours generously, downing the shot of whiskey. Slamming the empty glass down on the counter made her feel slightly better.

Hearing something outside, she goes to see what was going on. Several ghosts are hovering over Tom's body and putting a sheet over him. Eyes were cut out of the sheet. Madison has no idea where the sheet came from. Movement under the sheet draws her attention and she watches in amazement as Tom's body rises from the yard where it once lay. It turns and seems to stare at her. After a moment, all the ghosts shift and move in unison toward the wooden bridge, vanishing before her eyes.

FIERY MABLE

Rundown, sitting back from the road, a rural nursing home waits for its inhabitants. Whispers among many locals run rampant, as they would never send their own loved ones there. The building is one level; white, with paint peeling away its once youthful appearance. Wood rot was visible around the windows and the red bricks were crumbling. Multiple wings housed adults suffering from old age and numerous other afflictions. Sometimes, there are days where people who would show up for work would just look the other way, but not enough showed up that actually cared.

New to Horizon Elder Care, Damion was excited for the opportunity to earn a respectable living. He knew this place would never be fully staffed, so getting fired was not a concern. Quietly approaching his patient's room, he was lost in his thoughts. He was thinking that the added bonus of Mable not remembering him being there would work in his favor. He purposely chose to work here, knowing most patients here were dumped and forgotten.

Mable stirred, slowly waking up, and the terror in her eyes was clear, as Damion was caressing her. He ignored the fact that he knew she didn't enjoy their times together. When she saw Damion at her bedside, running his hand up and down her right arm, she wanted to run. She stiffened, but was so weak she could barely wiggle her toes, much less escape. He leaned in close, his lips nearly touching her ear, and whispered, "Mable, I look forward to getting to know you better."

"Please, just leave me alone!" Mable pleaded with him.

"Mable, I can't do that. Just relax and keep your eyes closed." Damion quickly unzipped his pants, grabbed Mabel by the legs, and pulled her close to him.

"Damion, *what are you doing*?" Evelyn, the RN with a

past that would make most people blush, asked as she came in to check on Mable. She arched an eyebrow, pursed her lips, and shot Damion a warning look.

"Damn it", he whispered to himself. Damion looked guilty as he answered, "Ummm, nothing. Just putting lotion on Mabel's legs, they were dry." He then turned and zipped up his pants, but not before Evelyn noticed and let her gaze linger. She liked what she saw - his tousled black hair, green eyes, and fit stature, standing at 6'3. His smile was something to die for.

"Uh, huh. Well, just get to Mr. Donnley's room. He needs help to go to the restroom."

"Fine. I'll be back soon." Damion responded, while staring at Mable and giving her a wink as well as a grin of unspoken promises to be kept between the two of them. Mable glared at Damion and then looked at Evelyn, pleading with her eyes.

Evelyn, catching Mable's eyes in a sideways glance, shook her head. "No, that's okay Damion. Just stay with Mr. Donnley tonight. John called in."

"Well, if you think so."

"I *definitely* think so. Get going before Mr. Donnley wets his bed. He will do it too, I promise." Evelyn was firm and needed him to follow directions, for once on this shift. Evelyn now stood at the foot of Mable's bed.

Mable's stress and fear seemed to evaporate as she struggled to open her mouth.

"Thank you." Mable said, in a quiet and feeble voice that cracked. She was a tall, regal lady, seventy-five years old. She was beautiful once, but the years had been unkind, as she is now frail and plagued with serious vascular dementia. Her life expectancy was only for a few more years.

"You're welcome, Mable. I'll make sure Damion isn't in your rotation schedule anymore, okay?"

Mable nodded her head in agreement, as she drifted off to sleep again after Evelyn administered a sedative. Evelyn knows she shouldn't give her a sedative in her IV, but she also knows how difficult Mable can be for Damion.

At the nurses' station, Damion was ending a phone call just as Evelyn walked up.

"She's all yours D. Make it quick."

Damion's grin spread across his face and he saw Evelyn take notice. He headed towards the Alzheimer wing at a brisk pace. After about two minutes, he reached the wing and buzzed himself in with his key card. As he was opening the door to Mable's room, he noticed another patient rummaging through Mable's clothes. *Well, that explains why her clothes are disappearing,* he thought with a snicker.

"Mandy, what *are* you doing here?"

"I'm looking for my blue blouse with tiny pink flowers. I thought it was in here somewhere." Clearly agitated, Mandy kept searching for her blouse in Mable's belongings.

"Mandy, those aren't your clothes. Please leave Mable's stuff alone, and get back to your room. It's room 220, remember? Okay, let's go. You don't want to wake her up now, do you?" Damion coaxed Mandy out of the room, and she shuffled along the corridor towards her own sleeping quarters.

Quietly shutting the door, he walked towards Mable. From his scrub pocket, he retrieved a scalpel. He pulled back the covers as she slept and lightly nicked her on her upper thighs. His heart raced, and he caught his excitement in his throat as bloody dots formed on the delicate surface of her paper-thin, aged skin. He leisurely ran his tongue over her thighs and savored the blood on his tongue. Closing his mouth and eyes, he moaned.

He backed up as Mable shifted her position in bed and was now sleeping on her side, facing the wall so her back was toward Damion. He reached over her and put his hand over her mouth. Slowly, Mable became restless and fluttered her eyes open. As he was about to end her life with a pillow, he heard a soft knock on her door and it opened with Mable's daughter appearing; her face stricken with confusion and alarm. " Can you please explain what you are doing to my mom?" Jenny asked, staring at Damion expectantly while the anger showed in her eyes.

"Oh, I was walking by on my rounds and I found another patient, Mandy, in here. I had to shoo her off. I noticed your mom was moving around a lot, and I went to her to see if she needed anything. I think she was having a nightmare. I was fluffing her pillows for her, to make her more comfortable." He was fidgeting and appeared uncomfortable around Jenny. "I'll let you visit while I continue my rounds."

Jenny glared at him as he left. "Mom, that was just weird. I don't think we can trust that guy."

"No, I don't believe we can. I feel...gross. I think I really need a bath."

"I'll talk to the RN in charge before I leave. I'll let you rest before dinner. Afterwards, I'll bathe you"

"I need a bath now, I feel gross." Mable whined, and flipped over on her back and with her bloodshot, sleep deprived eyes, looked around as if she were taking stock of her surroundings. It was obvious that she still felt threatened, even now that Damion had left.

"Is he gone? That ugly male nurse; he gone?"

"Mom, yes, yes, he's gone. He said he had rounds to take care of. We just talked about this, why?"

Mable looked down as she was about to explain, but she noticed blood on her sheets, her legs were bleeding.

"What the shit is this?!" Mable yelled and kicked off the covers in a panic.

"Mom, calm down. Looks like you probably scratched yourself."

"The hell I did!" Mable's eyes reflected a frenzied stare at her daughter.

"Mom, what's going on?"

"I don't know, but I think Damion is doing more than he should be." Fear dripped with her words as she whispered.

"Mom, let's change your clothes and sheets." Jenny yelled down the hall for the nurse.

"Evelyn, can you get us some clean sheets and band-aids? I'll put a clean nightgown on her after I bathe her."

Jenny gently took off the soiled and bloody night-gown, threw it on the floor, and quickly gave her mom a light sponge bath after Evelyn brought her the plastic bin with soap, a washcloth, and band-aids. Jenny had her cleaned up when Evelyn returned with clean sheets.

Several brown stains covered the new sheets, and Jenny glared at Evelyn as she stripped the bed. Mable was sitting in her adjustable recliner reading a magazine, but peered over it to watch the exchange between Evelyn and Jenny.

Jenny stared at Evelyn in disbelief, clearly not happy about the stained sheets that looked used and dirty.

"Evelyn, are you sure those sheets are clean? They look disgusting. I can put on some sheets that I brought from home. Just take those and I'll use mine, please."

"Fine, you can handle it. I'll be back after dinner." Evelyn left abruptly and seemed annoyed.

After Mable and Jenny had dinner and a lengthy conversation, Mable dozed off. Jenny decided it was time to go home, but she was going to speak with the nursing supervisor first.

Jenny called her daughter from her cell phone. "Sara, why don't you have dinner with your dad before his night shift tonight? I ate with your grandma."

"Sure, mom. Will you be home soon?"

"Yeah, probably like thirty minutes or so. I need to talk to a nurse first, then I'll head out. Love you."

"Okay, I'll grab dinner for dad and myself. Love you too."

Jenny put her cell phone in her purse after she talked to her daughter. She was unhappy with the care that her mom was receiving. She was going to report this place tomorrow, before Damion escalated into doing something even more horrific. Everyone in charge needed to know what he was really like.

Jenny cleaned up her mom's room, pulled the blanket up high under her chin, and kissed her on the head, while whispering how much she loved her, and that Sara would be in to see her tomorrow. Looking at her mom and feeling sadness bubble up to the surface because of all the things she wouldn't experience absolutely broke her heart. She knew she had little time left on this earth, but she wanted it to be peaceful. Nothing about this place screams peaceful. Even though her mom was rough around the edges, she knew she loved her family deeply. Sighing, she grabbed her things, put her belongings in her cross-body bag, and quietly shut the door behind her.

SHE HEADED TO THE NURSES' STATION. IT WAS A bit of a walk, and the fluorescent lights above flickered. She thought about how the lights were dimmer the further away from her mom's room and wondered how to get Damion fired. He needed to be out of here, and that was the only thing on her mind now. It was quiet, and there were no other visitors in sight. *Maybe the rumors are true about this place*, Jenny thought.

As she turned a corner in the hallway, she heard muffled voices. Glancing at the nurses' station, no one was there. Jenny wasn't surprised. Quietly, she creeped towards the doorway from which she heard the voices. The sounds echoed in the hallway, and she leaned against the wall to listen carefully. She heard the two nurses whispering, but she couldn't tell what they were saying. She accidentally put her hands on something sticky from the wall and pulled her hands away. It was like a soft, thin gossamer fabric, with tiny black spiders embedded in it. The more Jenny tried to get the spider web off of her, the quicker the newly hatched spiders moved and crawled up her arms. She was terrified of spiders and opened her mouth to scream. In order to avoid being discovered, she suppressed the urge to let the sound out. She accidentally bit her tongue in the process of brushing off the spiders and winced while hoping the pain subsided soon. Despite quickly brushing off the spiders, she could still feel them. She decided to peek around the corner into the nearby room since she couldn't hear their conversation, but suddenly stopped dead in her tracks. Remaining silent as she looked at what was before her proved to be difficult. Yet, sadly, she found her instincts proved right.

Jenny watched in horror as Damion was carving up the elderly woman, Mandy, who lived down the hall from her mom. He appeared to be skilled in his surgical endeavors. Jenny stepped back in the shadows of the hallway to ensure that she wasn't discovered and noticed that Evelyn was filming Damion. She took a few deep breaths and tried to calm her nerves. Mandy's blood was flowing freely from her wrists, hitting the cold linoleum tiles that every room had. The blood covered the white grout like small rivers heading to the mouth of the floor. He then moved towards Mandy's chest. He closed her eyes and slit her stomach and beyond with precision. Reaching in, he gingerly grabbed her intestines and held them for a moment. He purposely dropped them on the floor - blood spattered everywhere, including on Damion's uniform. Next, he then reached in for the liver. Carefully, he placed it in an ice chest on a table next to him. He had opened her chest cavity prior to Jenny watching them. With caution, he extended his hand into her chest and clutched her heart. Gently placing her heart in the ice chest, he looked over at

Evelyn asked, "Any other organs we need, or is it just the two?"

"I think the two will do for now. Let me video the ice chest so they see what they are getting."

Evelyn walked, avoiding the blood on the floor, to where the organs were and took a quick photo.

"This should be good enough for them. We will make the exchange tonight. They agreed to bring the cash. We split it, okay? Don't be greedy."

Laughing, Evelyn put her phone away and Damion grabbed her by the waist and pulled her close. He licked the scalpel and closed his eyes in obvious ecstasy.

"Let's go, I'm ready." Evelyn whispered. Damion grabbed Evelyn and pulled her even closer. Blood dribbled down his chin, but Evelyn didn't seem to care. They continued to passionately kiss and then they started to undress. When they were both sweaty and naked, Damion lifted Evelyn up and set her on the nearest countertop. Murder turned them on.

JENNY REALIZED MANDY WAS GUTTED LIKE AN animal. She thought that Mandy slowly turned her head while her eyes fell on her own and before the light slowly faded from her eyes, whispered, *help me*. Jenny's color drained from her face while she covered her mouth with her hands, momentarily forgetting about the spiders that had left lingering crawling sensations on her skin. It finally sank in what she had witnessed. Trying to hold it in didn't work. First, she dry-heaved, then she vomited on the floor in the hallway. She didn't know what to do. She had never been so scared and disgusted in her life.

She ran in silence back to her mom's room when she heard a sound behind her. When she turned the corner, she looked back and Evelyn and Damion were standing there with their bloody scrubs on. They looked at each other and their smiles slowly grew unnaturally large across their faces.

Evelyn stated calmly and loudly to Jenny, "That's right, *run.*"

As Evelyn followed her, she slipped and fell in the vomit, hitting her head on the floor as the sound reverberated in the quiet hallway. Damion bent down to see if Evelyn was okay.

Shaking Evelyn, he became frantic. "Evelyn, Evelyn, wake up!"

Evelyn remained unconscious.

Jenny didn't have to be told twice. With relief flooding her thoughts, she hurried back to her mom's room, grateful that she was safe. She frantically shut the door, moved the chair, and barricaded the door. She looked around the room for a weapon, yet couldn't find one.

"Fuck!" Jenny panicked.

She ran over to the window to see if she could crawl out. The window was covered with bars, like a prison. She saw she had a lighter that she'd used for the cozy new candles she had brought, so she lit the two she had placed in her mom's room. Candles were calming to her, so she stared blankly at them, completely transfixed. She didn't know what to do next. Her mom woke up.

"Jenny, what's going on?"

"Mom, I'm so sorry. I put you in this place and I didn't know the people here were fucking evil!"

"Jenny, you *didn't* know."

"Mom, they *killed* Mandy. We have to get out of here!"

"Jenny, look under the hidden panel inside my nightstand. There is a secret panel that the staff doesn't know exists since I brought the nightstand from home. A gun is in there. It's a small handgun, but it's loaded. Hand me the lighter and the hairspray that I know damn well you have in your purse. Take the lid off. We are going to kill these fuckers."

"*Mom*! We're trapped." Jenny cried.

"Shit, Jenny, please. Pull yourself together if you want to survive this."

They heard noises outside the room. The crazy, murderous staff was trying to get in. Jenny and Mable were as ready for them as they could be. Jenny dialed 9-1-1. She told them what had happened and agreed to keep them on the line. She set down her phone by the candles, leaving the operator online to listen and dispatch the appropriate agencies to Horizon Elder Care.

"Oh Mable, I'm here for your evening sponge bath and meds." Damion cooed in a long, drawn out manner. Jenny and Mable both rolled their eyes and could not believe the reality that had become theirs.

"Mother fucker, I already had my bath, and you don't need to stick me with no needle. Go on, get outta here. I don't need you guttin' me like a pig, like you did to poor Mandy!"

Jenny just remembered that she still felt like she had cobwebs and spiders moving up and down her arm. She grabbed a towel from the closet and brushed her arm off. The spiders had fortunately moved on, likely scurrying away into the shadowy crevices of the hallway.

"Ladies, just let us in. This will be over soon. The next shift arrives shortly, so we have to finish our rounds." Evelyn's agitation and concern about being caught were obvious in her voice.

"How's your head Evelyn? Maybe you should be seen

by a doctor. That was a pretty nasty fall." Jenny spoke with confidence, even though she was terrified.

Damion and Evelyn managed to move the chair that blocked the door, which now stood slightly ajar. They started to squeeze through, but Mable got up to spray them with hairspray and a lighter in their faces.

"Damn it Bitch! It looks like we are at an impasse Mable." They both barely had singed hair and their hands were slightly pink from the flames. They pushed their way completely in and were angry and ready for a fight.

"Evelyn, please, just let us leave." Jenny pleaded.

"Oh, now you know that can't happen." Damion spoke with evil in his eyes and sarcasm in his voice. He lunged for Jenny. She wasn't quick enough and dropped the gun. Evelyn saw it skitter across the floor and easily grabbed it. She held the gun and pointed it at Jenny. Her hands were shaking, as she had never held a gun before. Damion forcefully plunged the scalpel from his pocket into Jenny's chest, only it didn't go as deep as he had hoped. He jostled it around to increase her pain and enjoyed the expression of shock and sadness on her face.

Mable gasped and began wailing loudly and screaming at Damion to stop, "You evil fuck, leave her alone!"

She pointed the lighter and hairspray at him. He

looked amused and drove the scalpel deep into Jenny's neck this time after pulling it from her chest. Mable fired up the lighter and the hairspray and Damion was close enough to have his hair catch fire from the makeshift flamethrower. Mable turned to her right side and fired it again at him, catching his scrubs on fire. He let go of the scalpel, yelped in pain, and rolled around in an attempt to put the fire out. Evelyn was caught up in all the confusion and Damion grabbed her leg. With a reaction of pure instinct, she accidentally shot him in the face.

Mable gathered all her strength so she could get to Damion, then decided to take the scalpel that was stuck in Jenny's neck. She gently placed a towel on Jenny's wound.

"Jenny, hold the towel there as firmly as you can, and don't move it." Blood streamed beneath the towel as Jenny's strength waned.

Determined, Mable stood in front of Evelyn, pointed the flamethrower at her without fear, and set Evelyn ablaze. Evelyn, in her frenzy to put the fire out, dropped the gun. It landed in front of Mable. She picked it up, knowing there were more bullets left. She raised the gun and leveled it at Damion first, at close range, and pulled the trigger, aiming at his temple. Chunks of skull and brain matter hit the floor, and blood sprayed indiscriminately around the room. She then looked at Evelyn with her charred skin and scrubs that melted into her skin. It was impossible to tell where melted skin ended and melted scrubs began. Evelyn pleaded with her eyes, as her mouth was no longer distinguishable.

"No, Evelyn. You aren't going anywhere. You will die here, just like Damion. I'm just sorry you put the fire out. Any last words?"

Evelyn shook her head, finally accepting defeat. The damned didn't get an opportunity for redemption, and she knew she would not see the light in her final moments. Mable fired all the remaining shots at Evelyn, cutting her dying screams short. Drenched in indescribable fear and redemption, Mable was satisfied that Evelyn laid in a heap at her feet.

Voices from the hallway were becoming audible as they became closer and closer. Mable looked up at her door as she sat down on her bed. She threw the gun back in the nightstand. Rushing over to Jenny, she hoped to save her, but all life had already drained from her daughter. She wasn't cold to the touch yet, and she embraced her and rocked her back and forth like she did when she was young. Mable wept, as her heart shattered into a thousand pieces while cradling her baby. This left her feeling broken, with no reason to be on Earth anymore.

Mable gently laid Jenny down on the floor and covered her up with a blanket then pulled the flowers from her vase, placing them on top of the blanket. She whispered a quick prayer.

Setting the bed and curtains on fire was her doing, by accident, but she couldn't remember doing it. She stood back and watched in amazement as the blaze quickly erupted into an inferno.

Mable backed up and knocked into the end table with the lit candles. The candles fell over and a blanket by her chair that was hanging low on the floor caught fire. She was confused and remembered nothing about what had happened. She turned to leave her room as the fire was spreading throughout the room. Mable was searching for a way out because she couldn't remember where the exit doors were. She was shuffling down the hallway as something exploded behind her. Flailing her arms, she stumbled and fell to the floor. She screamed out in pain and desperation.

The nursing home was engulfed by the time the fire department and police officers arrived. When the fire trucks stopped, Jeremy jumped off and ran to the cops to ask if there was anyone inside. They let him know that they also just arrived and did not know who was there, but it didn't look like any survivors were likely.

Jeremy fell to his knees. "My wife, my wife!"

He sobbed as his fire company rained down gallons of water on the nursing home to put the flames out. The efforts would take time to get the fire manageable, and embers would burn for hours afterwards. Nothing was left that would be identifiable. Jeremy stood there and felt a chilling wind while something briefly held his hand. He felt and heard indistinguishable whispers in his ear. Shivering, he walked back to the fire truck, dreading the call he would have to make to tell his daughter Sara the news about her mom and grandmother. He was mentally preparing himself for the most challenging call of his life, thus far. The sky was peppered with stars in its inky darkness, and dawn was a few hours away. He wouldn't be able to keep her away, even though it was still considered the middle of the night by most standards. He knew this. Drying his tears and taking a few deep breaths, he made the call.

"Sara, it's Dad."

"Dad, what's up? It's late."

"Are you sitting down? I have some terrible news. There was a fire at the nursing home and it looked like there were no survivors."

"What? Didn't mom leave already? She was supposed to be home before now!"

"No, honey. She didn't make it home. Are you not home?"

Between crying jags, Sara responded, "I'm at Darren's

house. I wanted to see him before I went back to school. Dad, I'm on the way."

Jeremey couldn't argue or change her mind, he knew this much. He would wait for her. Darren would likely drive her. He was a good young man, and he knew he loved his daughter. He will have to step it up right now for Sara, so she could get through this.

There wasn't a summer breeze, yet Jeremy felt one near him again as he waited by the firetruck. He felt something touch his cheek and hold his hand again. If he didn't know better, he would think it was Jenny telling him that everything would be fine. He inhaled deeply as the breeze dissipated, and he was left with Jenny's perfume she spritzed herself with every morning. Tears sprung to his eyes, as memories of her flashed through his mind like a Viewfinder toy, clicking through each photo.

A truck rumbled in the distance and soon Darren and Sara were visible as they pulled up to a stop in front of the firetruck. Sara jumped out and ran towards her dad. She embraced him with such force that he stumbled back a bit. Darren got out and stood awkwardly next to his truck, not really knowing what to do, judging from his expression. Sara and Jeremy hugged each other, and tears streamed down their faces for several minutes. Darren then joined them after he gave them their privacy and a chance to talk briefly.

"Mr. Frost, I'm so sorry about your wife and mother-in-law. I'll do whatever I can to help."

"Thank you Darren. I appreciate that. Just take care of Sara." He gently squeezed Darren's shoulder in appreciation as he walked away to discuss everything with the fire investigators that were in the process of documenting the scene. One was taking photos and the other one was working on extensive notes. It was a grueling process, which Jeremy knew firsthand. The investigators, Nick and Eric, were discussing details as part of the building that was unstable, but still standing, collapsed and erupted in a secondary fire.

Sara stopped talking to Darren and looked at the nursing home and then looked at her father with eyes wide with worry. The firefighters in her dad's company quickly flooded the flames to extinguish them. Jeremy walked over to Sara and put his arms around her. As he did, more flames erupted and what looked like a silhouette of Mable could be seen from the fading flames. Sara gasped and looked at her dad. "Did you see that? Tell me I really saw what I saw!"

"I saw it, honey. Your mom's spirit is here, too."

A gust of wind circled them both and embraced them

before the skies opened up and a downpour was upon them.

PART THREE
WINTER

A HORROR IN THE DARK WOODS

Nestled in the heart of Deadwood, South Dakota sat the home of the Bender's. Rural, country, and far removed from city amenities. Life here provided limited access to success, plenty of boredom, and lots of opportunity for trouble. Life has been full of financial problems, marital issues, and a lack of fully present parenting. Audrey and Cooper have struggled with being parents and letting go of the past.

Audrey lost the love of her life during a horrific

surfing related accident, her sophomore year of college. Cooper was her rebound and she stayed with him for comfort as she didn't want to be alone. She loved him in her own way because they have children together. Her nightmares are kept at bay when she shares her bed with him, and accidents happen, as Audrey knows all too well.

She's had serious issues holding down a job due to her fragile mental health. Audrey has very little money and Cooper has even less. He likes to play video games all day; work is an afterthought, as are his kids. She knows she should leave him, but she isn't strong enough...yet.

"Hey, babe, guess what?" Cooper said.

"What, Cooper?" Audrey responds in the flat tone she uses when she is exasperated with him; which is most of the time.

"I talked to this older woman that I ran into at the grocery store. She said she would watch the kids for free for a few days since we are struggling right now and need time to look for jobs. I told her their names and ages already. She's the mother in-law of Doug, a guy I used to work with. Remember Doug? What do you think about her offer?"

"I think that it is crazy! We don't even know her. Does she have references? Why would a woman we don't even know want to watch our teenagers?" Audrey was losing patience with him.

"She did give me a resume, and she used to be a nanny. Here, you can call everyone on it." Cooper said.

"A resume? Seriously?"

"Well, she wrote down references on scratch paper from her purse, same thing." Cooper said.

Audrey looked at him with sheer disgust. She ripped the paper out of his hands and grabbed her cell phone from the counter to make the calls. Maybe proving him wrong would motivate him to find a job sooner, rather than later. She headed to their bedroom and closed the door. She sat on their bed that was comfortable, but well past its prime, like most stuff in their small home.

"Hi, Mrs. Henson, this is Audrey Bender, and my husband said you offered to watch our kids for us?" "Yes, I understand, that is so kind of you to offer. How many years of experience do you have? Ok, thirty years is significant. Yes, I'm going to call your references in a moment, then call you back. Thank you."

Audrey called the three references, and they were all glowing reviews. It put her at ease and gave her a bit of hope that she would have time to get a job and get her life on track. She wants nothing more than to be able to provide for her kids on her own.

"Mrs. Henson, it's Audrey again. Your references are great! Yes, we will take you up on that. I'd like for all of us to meet first, to make sure it's a good fit. The morning we drop them off, if we feel like it won't work out, we will call it off. Say hello to Doug for us. Ok, Mrs. Henson I'm happy you agree with that, thank you."

"DROP THEM OFF AT YOUR HOUSE? I'M NOT SURE about that, but I guess that makes sense. Thank you, and we will see you tomorrow." Avery clicked the red button on her iPhone to end the call.

After Audrey's phone call, she went back to the living room where Cooper was gaming and slamming beer after beer. Seeing that gave her even more motivation to turn her and her children's lives around. Clearly there would be no job hunting for Cooper today.

"Cooper, it's all set. We will drop them off at her house tomorrow after a quick meet and greet, and she will bring them home on Saturday. That gives us three days to hit the pavement and find something, even if it's seasonal."

Cooper responds, "Yep, sounds good."

"That means you *have* to look for a job too, since the unemployment money dries up next month. We have to work Cooper! It's December 19th as it is, that doesn't give us much time. I'm tired of being one step away from being destitute." Audrey angrily said.

Cooper was still engaged in the new game and was

beating his current opponents, shutting out everything she was telling him.

"Cooper!" Audrey yelled at him. She was getting so tired of him behaving like a child.

"What? I'm knee deep in this game, can't it wait?"

"Cooper, tomorrow morning we drop the kids off so we can job hunt. You better be ready by 8:30 in the morning!"

Cooper was still lost in his game, but managed a quick, dismissive, "Okay."

Audrey shook her head and then sat the kids down to explain to them what was going on.

"Mom, seriously?" Chris just couldn't believe what he was hearing. That's a load of shit mom! Just let us stay home, please?"

"Chris, first of all, please watch your language. Second, it gives us more time to focus on applying for positions that can lead to something more. I have to revamp my resume and shop for a nice interview outfit. I need the time."

"Oh? Is dad doing all that too? I mean, he just plays games and drinks beer, and is the laziest adult I know! It's embarrassing, mom. Kids at school are always talking about him," Chris says in an irritated voice.

"Honey, I know. The time will also give me a chance to talk to him about everything, and you and

Callie really don't need to be around when that happens. He might not handle it well, since I'm basically giving him an ultimatum." Audrey spoke with authority.

She was worried about how Chris would process that information. He is very intuitive and mature for his age. Audrey feels extremely blessed in that sense. Now, how Cooper will take that, she has no idea.

Cooper drains the family resources for his gaming purchases and add-ons while chugging his weight in beer at home, if he isn't slamming beers at the local pub. That would be how kids at school would know about him. Unbeknownst to him, some of the younger gamers are friends with Chris. The pub owner has a boy that plays too, namedSam. He is in the same sophomore class as Chris. Deadwood isn't exactly a bustling big city where someone can easily disappear.

"Callie, I need to talk to you, come here for a minute!" Audrey yelled out at Callie's door, and she could feel the loud music vibrating as she stood outside her door and knocked.

"*What is it, mom!*" Callie was easily annoyed with anyone interrupting her music, or for any reason at all, for that matter.

Callie loves the 90's grunge scene and dresses like it too. Audrey doesn't mind hearing the music, just not as loud. Finally, Callie opens the door with an attitude that could give any teenage girl a run for her money.

"Cali, tomorrow morning I'm dropping you and your brother off to a nanny's house so your dad and I can job hunt. We leave at 8:30 in the morning. Her name is Mrs. Henson, she's older and seems very nice. I'm hoping you will be respectful?"

"Whatever." Callie states rudely.

"Callie, enough of the attitude! Please go pack for the three days you'll be gone. After Mrs. Henson drops you off Saturday morning, we will go to breakfast at Lee Street Station Cafe, okay? I'm getting dinner started, you want to help?"

"Um, no." Callie rolled her eyes at her mom, and stormed out of the hallway.

She slammed her bedroom door shut a few seconds later. Audrey sighed and hoped that the attitude issue would improve soon. She headed to the kitchen to make dinner. She thought she would make a nice meal before they had a hectic few days ahead and were separated from each other.

Fortunately, dinner was enjoyable for all, which was hit or miss on any given night. Audrey made a pesto vegetable lasagna, garlic toast, and a Caesar salad. No one complained about the food, which was a family milestone.

"Alright, everyone needs to get ready for bed, we have a busy morning ahead!" Audrey spoke in a motivated manner to get everyone out of the post dinner food coma.

Chris and Callie went to their bedrooms. Soon afterwards, the lights no longer showed underneath the crack beneath their doors. Audrey breathed a sigh of relief that she wouldn't have a bedtime battle tonight, at least not with the kids.

"Cooper, can you help me clean up the kitchen? We need to get ready for tomorrow morning and get to bed at a decent hour tonight."

"Audrey, come on...I need to finish this round, I don't want to die in this game at the hands of a 16-year-old gamer!"

"Cooper, let's go, in the kitchen *now*."

Audrey felt ridiculous having to use a parental tone with her immature and lazy husband. What on earth did she ever see in him? Audrey looked at him with utter disdain and disgust. The chances of this marriage surviving much longer didn't look good.

THE NEXT MORNING, ALL FOUR WERE UP AT 6:30 a.m. to get ready for the day. The kids finished packing while Avery prepped her resume folder and practiced her interview responses and smile in her bathroom.

"Mom, what are you doing?" Callie asked while she stifled a laugh.

"I'm practicing applying for jobs and smiling in the mirror."

Cooper was dressed for success this morning. He poured himself a cup of coffee before mayhem ensued. He left to gas up the car, had the address to Mrs. Henson's house, and loaded the kids' bags in the trunk when he returned. He felt proud of himself now. This is the most adult thing he has done in quite some time.

"Callie, Chris, let's go!" Audrey yelled out to the kids.

The kids sluggishly got in the backseat of the 2016 Kia Sorento that Audrey's parents bought her so she would have a reliable car for herself and the kids. They really didn't care for Cooper much, for obvious reasons. Cooper started the car, waited for everyone to get in, and they drove the ten minutes to Mrs. Henson's house. It was a cute little home with nice curb appeal, and as they got out of the car, they noticed the beautiful Christmas lights and the tree in the window. Audrey thought about her Christmases at her grandparents' house every year and a wave of emotional nostalgia caught in her throat. She cleared her throat and got out of the car.

"Ok let's be on our best behavior, okay?" She looked at her kids and, then at Cooper, who lacked social graces at times.

Mrs. Henson opened the door with a warm and friendly smile plastered across her face. She resembled *Mrs. Doubtfire* in personality and body, but her hair was stylish with an above the shoulder layered bob and expensive red and gold *Fendi* glasses. She welcomed the family inside and offered them fresh coffee and pastries. "Please have a seat in the sitting room, and I'll bring a tray of coffee and pastries."

"Mom, do we really have to stay here for three days?" Callie whispered.

"Callie, yes. You will survive, I promise," rolling her eyes at her daughter as she spoke.

Chris just sat there quietly, not knowing what to say. Cooper had an annoyed look on his face, but at least kept his snarky comments to himself.

The home reflected picturesque Christmas decor, resembling a gingerbread cottage with all kinds of desserts and candies in every room. It was cozy and quaint, and looked like a magazine cover with modern Pinterest inspiration. Reds, greens, and golds everywhere, including the kitchen. The sitting room had a fireplace that was burning brightly, which sets the tone for a cozy morning.

Slowly waddling in from the kitchen, Mrs. Henson brought the breakfast tray and set it on the coffee table. "Pour your coffee and grab a little or a lot of the breakfast carbs of your choice." Mrs. Henson said with a little chuckle.

"Thank you so much, this is really kind of you. Here is the list with our cell numbers, their preferred foods, and a friend's number in case of an emergency. They aren't allergic to anything, so you're good there." Audrey said.

"Audrey, that is wonderful and so helpful. I appreciate it. I have some fun Christmas activities planned for them, they will be busy and have guaranteed loads of fun!" Mrs. Henson spoke enthusiastically.

Chris gives Mrs. Henson a side-eyed glance as he sat with doubt and an uncomfortable feeling. No one noticed.

Cooper spoke up for the first time, "Well, we need to head out and get started on that job search." He stood up and looked at Audrey, encouraging her to leave now.

"I will drop them off Saturday at 9:00 a.m. as discussed. Don't worry, they will be fine." Mrs. Henson said warmly.

Mrs. Henson followed Audrey and Cooper to the door

and firmly shut out the cold after they left. She sighed deeply and proceeded to head to the sitting room where the teenagers were. She hoped her plans would go accordingly. She texted her friend, whom she expected over in a couple of hours. She assumed the two kids would not give her problems since they were quiet and sullen.

Chris and Callie were given the grand tour of the small home. Two bedrooms, one belonging to Mrs. Henson with her own ensuite, and the other had two twin beds decorated for Christmas with twinkle lights and snowman bedding, adorned with decorative pillows placed on top of the bedspreads. The bathroom Chris and Callie would use was down the hall towards the sitting room. They were drawn to the covered back porch area that had a spectacular view of the wooded area behind Mrs. Henson's home. It was renovated for indoor use and now had central heat. Although the backdoor and windows were drafty with a chill in the air, it was still the best room with a view. Comfortable Christmas blankets lay over the back of each loveseat, positioned facing the woods into the unknown and desolate parts of Deadwood. Callie and Chris stared outside, lost in thought, until Mrs. Henson came in and interrupted them.

"Well there you two are! My friend is here, and we are

building gingerbread houses together, won't that be fun? Mrs. Henson said.

THE TWO TEENS LOOKED AT EACH OTHER IN defeat and Chris said, "Sure, is it a contest? What do I win if mine is the best?"

"Oh, well the four of us can vote on it to decide. Now let's head to the kitchen table. I have cocoa and Christmas cookies ready to enjoy while we design our gingerbread houses." Mrs. Henson said as she ushered the teens in towards the kitchen.

"Chris and Callie, this is Mr. Hinkle. He has been my neighbor and friend for twenty years. Won't you say hello?"

Both teens shook hands with Mr. Hinkle and said hello respectfully. Cooper had an uneasy feeling about him.

The four of them sat around the table with hot chocolate steaming through the whipped topping and two perfectly decorated sugar cookies on each plate. They both ate a cookie quickly and drank the hot chocolate. All four of them began to decorate the small gingerbread houses already constructed with gingerbread and icing. Tons of toppings were in the center of the table, like a buffet ready to be eaten.

Callie spoke up first, "So, who is the judge of the gingerbread houses? I mean if all of us have one, that isn't really fair, is it?"

"Well," Mrs. Henson started, "My church friends will come over tomorrow night and they will decide. I just texted them, so it's already been arranged. The winner chooses what's for dinner tomorrow night, and the losers will clean up! How does that sound?"

"Not exactly what I was thinking, but ok." Callie said with a quizzical look on her face.

Chris had scarfed down his two cookies and was on a third, while drinking the last of his hot chocolate. "Man, I'm getting tired, that's weird. It's only like 4 p.m. and I feel like I do after a day at school and hockey practice."

"Yea, I feel pretty beat too. Strange we feel that way at the same time, huh?" Callie spoke with an upbeat light-hearted tone.

"It's probably been a mentally draining day, considering what you've been through." *And what you don't know you'll go through soon,* Mrs. Henson thought, in a sinister way with a smirk on her face; only Mr. Hinkle noticed.

"Why don't you head to your bedroom and get ready

for bed. We will continue the Christmas activities tomorrow morning. How does Cherry Belgium waffles with cinnamon apples sound for breakfast?" Mrs. Henson asked.

"Yum," both teens said in unison. They looked at each other and laughed.

As the kids were headed to their room to get ready for bed, Mr. Hinkle and Mrs. Henson were deciding the next phase of their plan.

"The added Benadryl in the hot chocolate was a nice touch, Mr. Hinkle."

"Why thank you Mrs. Hinkle. Oh, I mean Mrs. Henson." They both laughed.

They prepped the things they needed to tie up both kids to the rails on the beds they were sleeping in. They had electrical tape for their mouths and rope for their hands and feet. After the kids were asleep, they would make sure they were secure for the quick transition to the cellar early in the morning.

At 3:00 a.m. Cooper awoke, feeling groggy and fighting a mild headache. He felt something on his face and subsequently he noticed that his arms and legs were bound by ropes and he was also gagged with a sock and tape. Thankfully the rope wasn't as tight as he thought it would be.

Old people are not that strong, he thought.

He quickly got out of the rope binding. Slowly, he tore off the tape from his mouth, spit the sock out on the floor, and began to free his sister too. She stirred, opened her eyes, and nearly screamed, but Cooper was able to stifle her scream long enough to set her free.

"Callie, get your clothes on over your pajamas and then put your shoes on. We've gotta get out of here *now.*"

"What happened Cooper? Why were we tied up and stuff?"

"Callie, I don't know why, but we need to go before they see us. We need to leave through the sliding glass door at the back patio. *Quietly,*" he whispered.

COOPER AND CALLIE SHIVERED AS THEY TRUDGED through the snowy secluded woods near the house they'd escaped from. "Cooper! I can't feel my feet, I'm so cold!" Callie spoke, with chattering teeth.

Cooper was agitated because he couldn't believe their parents would abandon them and leave them with such psychotic people. He was feeling foolish for thinking that their parents would ever pull it together.

"Callie, there isn't much I can do about that, I'm cold too."

His lips were dry and cracked, and blood started to dot the outline of his mouth. They estimated they'd been walking for nearly an hour, but they couldn't keep track of the exact time without a watch. The snow drifts along the country road were only going to get bigger as the snow fall increased and fell heavier throughout the early morning hours. Chris put his arms around Callie's shoulders and rubbed them vigorously to warm up his little sister.

What 12 and 16-year-old would ever survive being stranded in the middle of nowhere, Cooper thought.

As they were beginning to start walking towards town, they saw smoke rising in the distance in the early morning sky. Even though Cooper was confused about what direction they needed to go, he thought it might be near their home.

"Callie look! There's chimney smoke! It doesn't look too far. Let's go get help and warm up. They wouldn't turn away innocent abandoned kids, right?"

He smiled a weak smile at his sister, trying to give her hope and a promise of warmth. They picked up their pace in hopes of reaching the nearby home soon.

In a dark wooded area nearby, a low growl could be

heard near the kids. Callie and Chris looked at each other, terrified. The growling grew in intensity.

"Callie! Climb that tree, now!"

As Chris was giving her a lift, a hot searing pain was felt throughout his ankle. He got Callie in the tree safely, but was being attacked by a large wolf. It appeared hungry. It wore a dull coat of gray fur and had an unrelenting fury in its eyes.

"Shoo! Get off me!" Chris screamed.

He picked up a nearby large and sturdy branch that had a sharp and jagged edge to it and drove it into the wolf's right eye multiple times. The wolf yelped in pain, then started whimpering. It ran into the woods as quickly as it had run out towards him. Chris noticed the wolf tore his ankle open; the blood was flowing freely, and strings of flesh were hanging. Chris helped Callie out of the tree, not an easy task now that he was injured. They began to walk to the nearby homes. They hoped to find shelter, food, and a friendly face to help them.

In the distance they could hear wolves howling and muffled voices yelling for them. Mrs. Henson and Mr. Hinkle had realized they'd escaped. The teens were frightened and broke into a run. Well, Chris *tried* to run. It was more like a hop step movement, but it was quicker than if he walked. They got closer to the home with the chimney releasing puffy gray clouds. This was the house the siblings had hoped to reach and get help. As they neared the front door, they knew it wasn't their home, but thought maybe it was close by.

Chris knocked on the door, holding his breath in anticipation of being let in. A teenage girl answered the door. Her name was Nicole and she was from their school. He wanted to skulk away and hide his embarrassment.

"Chris, um, what a surprise." She looked him up and down and noticed his sister too. Then her line of sight landed on his ankle and its terrible injury.

"Hey Nicole, can we come in? We have a situation that's serious."

"Yea, I see that. Let me grab you a towel for your ankle. I'll get my dad too since he is a doctor." Nicole let them into the entryway and started to leave to get her dad.

Chris gently grabbed Nicole's arm. "You don't understand, that is not what I'm talking about. We barely escaped Mrs. Henson's house, her and her guy friend had us bound and gagged."

"Chris what are you talking about, there is no Mrs. Henson that lives around here." Nicole looked at Chris like he had lost his mind.

"I'll be right back with my dad."

Callie sat on the stairs that lead upstairs, where she

assumed all of the bedrooms were. Nicole and her dad walked back to the door from the living room area where Dr. Willow's office was also located.

"Chris, Callie, nice to meet you both." Dr. Willow gently took Chris's ankle to look at the injury. "Well, it's serious if not treated, but I can get you fixed right up. Why don't you go sit on a chair in the kitchen and I'll get the supplies that I need to help you."

Dr. Willow went to grab an antiseptic, gauze, antibiotics, scissors, a needle, and dissolvable sutures. After Chris was fixed up to the best of Dr. Willow's capability at home, he asked Chris and Callie to tell him what happened. They shared their story and as they were finishing up, a loud forceful knock could be heard from the front door. Callie and Chris looked at each other and begged Mr. Willow to not tell them where they were. They wanted to call their parents.

When Mr. Willow answered the door, he assured the elderly couple that he hadn't seen their grandchildren. He closed the door and locked it. He then went into the living area where the kids were now huddled. There were no windows in that area of the house, so they were safe.

"Ok kids, they are gone. They said they were looking for their grandchildren. I presume that is you?" Mr. Willow asked.

"I guess, but they aren't our grandparents. We don't have grandparents that live here." Chris said.

Callie asked, "Can we call our mom?"

"Of course. I'll get my cell phone." Dr. Willow said.

The lights began to flicker and then went completely out. The teenagers all gasped at once in fear.

"Nicole, you take them to your room and lock the door. Do not come out unless I tell you to. Go now!"

"Ok, dad." Nicole said while standing, and Chris and Callie stood up with her and followed her to her bedroom.

The kids stayed in Nicole's dark room. The shades were drawn as well as the curtains, so Nicole lit a couple of candles so they wouldn't be shrouded in the darkness and terrifying shadows that could haunt a child's imagination.

Chris said, "Nicole, I'm really sorry about this."

"It's not your fault. I just hope the police get here soon." Nicole stated softly.

"Did your dad call the police? I didn't hear him talk to anyone." Callie said.

"Oh, I don't know. I just thought–" She was interrupted by a loud banging sound and then an even louder thud.

The kids were scared as the volume of the noises as well as their anxiety increased. Nicole's bedroom door began shaking, then it flew open and was nearly ripped off its hinges. Hungry wolves entered Nicole's bedroom. All three of them screamed as loudly as they could. The wolves hung together like pack animals do, yet the one alpha leader had an eye injury and couldn't see out of it. Chris immediately knew it was the one that attacked him. The wolf let out a low growl as a warning. Nicole's dad finally showed up and loaded a full clip into the handgun, firing at all three wolves. He shot all of them point blank in the head.

"Let's go! Now!" Dr. Willow shouted at the three teenagers.

They all scrambled to their feet and flew out of that bedroom as quickly as they could, except for Chris. He was a little slower due to his injury, but made it out of the bedroom, and then out of the house, soon after the others.

Dr. Willow had his SUV revving and the heater blasting while gesturing for the kids to hurry. They all jumped in and were ready to go. Fortunately, there were snow tires on the SUV so it could maneuver easily on the snow and icy roads. Chris thought they were on their way to Deadwood's downtown where they could get to the town's hospital.

They had been driving for about ten minutes when Chris noticed that they were on the street that Mrs.

Henson lived on. "Dr. Willow, this is the street that the bad old people live on. Why are we here?"

"Cooper, don't worry about it."

Dr. Willow soon pulled up to the familiar house that Callie and Chris barely escaped from earlier. Confusion and terror shone in their eyes.

"Noooo, please Dr. Willow, don't leave us here! Please! They are terrible people; they tried to kill us!" Chris was begging and pleading while Callie was sobbing in the backseat next to Nicole.

"Sorry Chris, we had a deal, and they need to keep their end of it." He then brought out a syringe he had kept hidden, and plunged it carefully into Chris's forearm. Chris was soon drowsy and trying to fight sleep. Shortly after the shot he was out like a light.

"Callie, I'm sorry, I must do the same to you. You'll wake up soon, I promise." He gently added the sedative to Callie's arm, and she soon drifted into a troubled slumber.

"Nicole, stay here and don't move."

"Dad, what is going on? Why would you do that to them? They don't deserve this!" She started to cry.

"I know you don't understand, but I'll explain later. Stay here, I'll be right back."

Dr. Willow eased out of the SUV and went to the

front door of the Hinkle's. Mr. Hinkle answered the door. "Ah, yes. You have the kids I presume?"

"Of course. You know we're really running out of kids to use for this experiment of yours. This has to stop. These kids didn't do anything wrong." Dr. Willow stated.

They both carried the two kids into the spare room and placed them on the beds. As they were talking, they headed towards the front door. They spoke for at least thirty minutes.

"The dad of these two received a nice sum of money, so I don't expect to hear any complaints about it from the parents." Dr. Hinkle said, matter of factly.

"Does the mom know? I doubt very seriously Audrey would let anything happen to her children, if she even knows about this!" Dr. Willow was getting heated.

"I don't know, and honestly, I don't really care. You can just go. I don't need you tonight. I'll call you in the morning. Remember, this stays fucking quiet, do you understand me, Dr. Willow?"

"Yes, I understand." Dr. Willow turned to go back to his car, back to his daughter. He had a few more things to say before he left. He turned one last time to discuss the situation,

In the meantime, Chris woke up and read a file hidden in the spare room where he and his sister were sleeping. The file was on missing children that were harvested for body parts and organs, but the kicker was the kids suffered from mutilations and torture. They weren't put under anesthesia or even murdered quickly, because Dr. Hinkle enjoyed the children's pain and suffering. The innocence of children and the sinister nature of Dr. Hinkle made Chris nearly nauseous with disgust. By killing Dr. Hinkle, he would save lives, he hoped and reasoned.

Chris crept silently down the hallway while the doctors continued their heated discussion. He then fired two consecutive gunshots and hit Dr. Hinkle in the back. Dr. Willow, with eyes widened with surprise, turned to the front door to escape. Chris had taken Dr. Willow's gun without him even noticing that it was gone during the drive over. It was obvious that Dr. Willow didn't care that he no longer had possession of the gun.

"Get your sister and let's go. I'll drive you home. Surely your parents will be home on a Friday night." Dr. Willow said, as he looked down at the blood pooling around Dr. Hinkle on the floor.

They both went to get Callie from the spare bedroom. Dr. Willow picked her up and carried her to his car, Chris following closely behind. As the front door slammed shut, they could hear the screams of Mrs. Hinkle mourning the death of her twisted husband and vowing revenge. She looked outside to see who was leaving.

Shock was not one of the feelings she had, but a deep-seated hatred for Dr. Willow and that damn brat, Chris.

DRIVING THE BENDER KIDS HOME WAS A QUIET experience since Callie was still sleeping, Nicole was in shock, and Chris was feeling a whirlwind of emotions he couldn't even express; not one of them. Dr. Willow was numb to everything that had transpired. He soon realized that he accidentally mixed up the sedatives and gave Callie the heavier dose. His thoughts traveled to a place just as dark as the isolated road he was driving on. He never meant to get involved with Dr. Hinkle, but he'd found out about the things that he kept locked up in the dark recesses of his own mind. If Nicole found out about what else he had done, she would never speak to him again. He already lost his wife; he didn't want to lose his daughter too.

When they pulled into the driveway next to the Kia, Chris had never felt so relieved and happy to be home. He got out of the car, adjusted the gun in the front of his pants, and made sure his shirt hung over it to hide it from view.

Dr. Willow helped Callie out of the car with Chris's help. Nicole just sat there, still in shock and sadness in the passenger side front seat. She didn't know what to do or think.

As Dr. Willow and the Bender kids approached the door, Cooper noticed that there was a commotion in the front of the house and he peered out of the front windows. He got up and opened the front door with a look of utter disbelief. He couldn't believe his kids were there. He felt dizzy, like his entire world was about to implode.

"Hi, oh, what's going on?" Cooper asked innocently.

"Cooper, stop your bullshit. You know what's going on, only it didn't happen, so now what?" Dr. Willow said.

Chris looked really confused about their exchange. "Dad? What's going on?"

"Nothing son, everything is fine. Take your sister to her room. Dr. Willow, please keep your voice down, my wife is asleep in our bedroom."

Dr. Willow began to raise his voice, "Is she really? You mean you didn't sell her to the highest bidder like you did your own children?"

"Dr. I have no idea what you are talking about!"

"Remember Dr. Hinkle and the deal you made with his wife that was posing as Mrs. Henson? The one-hundred thousand dollars you pocketed? Where is the money? Come on Cooper, *where is it*?"

"Fine, so what. The kids would have been fine. It's not a big deal."

"You idiot! He *murders* the children; he dismembers them and does it slowly to watch them suffer. There is no mercy where he is involved. He might be dead anyway. He was shot before we showed up." Dr. Willow said.

Chris stood there in the living room and heard it all. Tears slowly streamed down his cheeks and pooled on his shirt near his neckline. "Dad? You sent Callie and I off to be murdered for money?" He pulled the gun from his waistband and pointed the gun at his dad.

Audrey heard the commotion and rushed out of bed. She went to the living room where she saw her son holding her husband at gunpoint. "What is going on he–" she didn't finish what she was saying before a single gunshot landed dead center in Cooper's chest.

Cooper stumbled back and collapsed onto the floor. Blood was spreading over his shirt and splattered on Dr. Willow's face.

Audrey screamed.

Chris didn't mean to shoot his dad to kill him, he just wanted to hurt him. He looked at the gun in his hands and looked around the room and dropped the gun to the floor. It made a clunking sound as it landed on the floor and slid near Audrey. Fortunately, it didn't go off. He put his head in his hands and sobbed harder than he ever had in his life.

"Mom, I'm so sorry, I'm sorry, I'm sorry." He continued to weep for what seemed like an eternity. He knew he had to pull himself together before the cops showed up.

Audrey called 9-1-1. It was nearly ten minutes before the emergency vehicles and local police knocked on the front door. The crime scene took hours and it was nearly dawn before everything was wrapped up for the time being. The investigating officers asked if they could speak to Callie. Audrey went to get her. She peeked in and saw that she was still sleeping. She decided to go ahead and wake her up so she could be questioned and get it over with. Audrey gently shook her, and she would not stir.

"Callie!" "Wake up Callie! Please!" Audrey was screaming and the officers quickly came into the bedroom. The EMT's tried to revive her, but she was cold to the touch and didn't have a pulse. She had been gone for hours. Audrey continued screaming into the chest of an officer that was trying to console her. She sobbed for what seemed like an eternity as Chris looked on from the doorway, quietly crying alone.

A TWISTED MALEVOLENT CHRISTMAS

PROLOGUE

Steve scrambled and tried to escape as the evil Santa grabbed him. Steve's friends were dead at the hands of creatures that were everything nightmares are made of. He whimpered as Santa grabbed him with both hands and slammed him against the wall.

"You will take my place. I can't do this anymore!"

Santa opened his mouth wide and bit long and hard

into his neck and sucked the blood that streamed from his bite marks.

"*What did you do to me*?" Screaming and crying simultaneously as Steve's tears streamed down his cheeks.

He soon felt weak and fell to the floor in a crumpled mess. He slept for what seemed like an eternity. When he awoke, Santa and the creatures were gone, but a Santa suit remained. A note drenched in blood lay next to him.

It's your turn. It wasn't my choice, and it's not yours either. Put the suit on and everything will make sense. ~Santa

TWO YEARS LATER...

Harbor Curiosities was a unique antique store catering to people of all ages. Business had increased since Christmas was right around the corner, and patrons were hunting for difficult to find toys. The last sale of the evening was to a gentleman that had a likeness to Santa Claus, but he smelled like cigars, not cookies. He pushed a kid holding a board game out of the way as he came inside the store. The boy stumbled, but caught himself.

"Hey asshole, watch it!" The teenager glared at him as he left.

He chuckled at the teen boy and brushed it off.

Outside, as the boy was crossing the street, cars screeched, and a loud thump could be heard in the toy store. Greg, the store owner, ran to the door and gasped. The boy was hit by a cab, and it was clear he didn't survive. The board game was scattered all over the road and the teen was crushed under the tire with his head barely visible. Greg called 9-1-1 and hoped it would be taken care of quickly.

That can't be good for business, he thought.

The vile Santa with his red suit that was form fitting and worn, glowered with a sinister twinkle in his eyes. His teeth looked more canine than human, and he seemed unbothered by the death of the teen. He paid cash for the toys and board games he bought in a rush. As he was leaving, he paused with the door open and stared at Greg with disdain. He laughed as he shut the door, leaving a frigid draft and a flurry of snowflakes in his wake. Greg rushed to the door and locked up so he could head home soon. Greg's personality didn't allow for him to be very assertive. His wife was better at that than he was. He was grateful that his work day was over, as he was tired and wanted to get home. The holiday season always took so much from him every year, especially his time. Beginning his closing chores, he tried to get them done quickly.

Dust covered the large, ancient, and worn black book

Greg noticed near his register. He thought maybe it was from the book section of the store, but he didn't put it there. His wife co-owns the store and knows more about what merchandise is valuable, vintage, and where it goes. He reached to grab it, and he placed it on top of the counter where he usually did his paperwork. His eyes fell on the title, *Santa's Naughty List*. He chuckled. Wiping off the dust that was covering the book, he then opened it. The naughty list was organized by year, with the latest list of names for 2024. There were numbers after each name, denoting the ages of the names listed. No children were listed, as everyone was over 18 in the book. The book was comprehensive, alphabetized, and had a respectable girth.

Adults only, is this fiction I wonder? thought Greg.

He quickly flipped to the page with the last name Winters. He didn't see his name or his wife's name, which was a relief. He packed up his briefcase and decided to take the naughty list book home with him. He wasn't positive where the book came from, but if he were a betting man, he'd say the festive guy in red forgot it. He decided he'd bring it back tomorrow when he opened his store. This would definitely sell for a premium if it doesn't belong to him. Now that he was thinking about it, a beautiful porcelain doll with fiery red hair was brought in yesterday. His wife put it on the shelf in the doll section where the toy room was located. It looked familiar, like they had owned it before. He'd have to remember to ask her about it. He decided to open at noon tomorrow since Sunday was his "short" day; he only had his store open until four o'clock. He locked up and headed home in his Mercedes, to spend time with his wife Mia.

AFTER DINNER, GREG AND MIA CUDDLED UP ON the couch to watch a Christmas movie. Greg decided to show Mia the book he found at work. He was a hard working man. Middle aged and a bit overweight. Thick dark brown hair and pasty skin. Medium height and build and dashing good looks in his younger years caught the attention of Mia when they met. She was still beautiful and sought after by other men. Greg knew how lucky he was.

"I found this left by someone that came into my toy store today. Isn't this crazy? It's like a naughty list of all the adults. Is it ours, or did someone leave it?"

"Seriously? Let me see it. This doesn't look familiar, I don't think it's ours. Did you happen to look up our names?"

"Yeah, we're not in it though."

"That's good. Should we look up people we know?"

"I don't know, that seems intrusive. Ignorance is bliss in my world."

"Look up people you know, but lost touch with, see if they are listed."

"Mmm, not a bad idea, let's see…"

Greg started to flip through pages, looking for his college buddy that had passed away.

"Okay, I found Steve here. It has his death date here too. I wonder what he did to get on this list?" Greg was pointing at it for Mia to take a look.

"No idea. It doesn't give any specifics about that for anyone on the list, it looks like."

Mia was thinking about how she was grateful she wasn't on the list. Not that she would ever deserve to be. They continued to flip through the book and noticed others that were deceased as well.

MIA AND GREG DECIDED THEY WOULD TURN IN for the night. They quickly got ready for bed, as they were exhausted. Sleep soon found Mia, and she softly snored as Greg tossed and turned. Eventually he was able to fall asleep, even with the events of the day running through his mind on repeat. Greg stirred in his sleep as thumps on the roof became louder and more persistent, with thunderous vibrations. He bolted upright in his bed. Mia shifted and mumbled something, but went back to sleep.

"What the fuck *is* that?" Greg whispered to himself.

He got out of bed, put his slippers on, and swiftly went downstairs. He abruptly halted at the foot of the stairs when he heard noises coming from the living area near their fireplace. Colorado in December requires frequent use of the fireplace, so embers still burned from earlier in the evening.

"I know you're there, you can show yourself. We need to talk." Santa spoke in a whisper.

The creepy Santa was in his living room and this terrified him. He had scraggly, layered, white hair, a long scruffy beard, and wrinkles around his fiery bloodshot eyes. His teeth were slightly yellowed, his incisors longer and sharper than most people's. He had a cigar hanging out of his mouth, which he promptly flicked into the fireplace.

"Why are you in my house? Asked Greg. Santa rushed at him and put his hands over his mouth.

" I have a job to do. You won't want to help me, but

you *will*." He hissed at Greg and took his hand off of his mouth.

Greg whispered, "This isn't real. This isn't real. This isn't–"

"Shut up and listen. Santa was irritated and his mouth was extremely close to Greg's neck. He smelled Greg and poked his neck with one of his razor sharp nails. It drew a small dot of blood and Santa swiped it with his pointer finger and licked it clean. He sighed deeply and seemed more calm.

Greg was fearful to even speak again. He just stood there.

"I'll be in touch. Keep my book for now." He waved his open hand across the pages and Greg and Mia's names appeared in a golden glittery color, then quickly changed to a dingy, faded black.

"Greg, maybe, just maybe, the two of you will survive this. Well, I have more stops to make, but like I said, I'll be in touch."

"Wait, you look familiar, do I know you?" Greg spoke quietly.

"Sort of, in the past." Laughing at Greg.

With that, he quietly left through the front door while Greg was left completely confused and terrified about what just happened. He looked out the window. Santa picked up something large from the snowy front yard. He bit into its neck, ripping out skin and consuming as much blood as he possibly could. When he was finished, he slung it over his shoulders like a sack of potatoes. Upon closer inspection, he realized Santa was carrying a body. He dropped the body to the ground and three shadows appeared out of nowhere and hovered over the carcass. They devoured the remains at a rapid pace and he could hear the slightest of animal noises as the woman was being feasted upon. He covered his mouth so as to not give away his location inside the house. He was now scared that those things would come inside. He looked at the clock on the DVR and it was 4:00 am. Heading back to bed was his best course of action. He had to get more sleep to get a better handle on the situation. To be able to tell Mia in a diplomatic way so she would believe him, he needed to be sharp. As he mulled over ways to present this to Mia, he silently and stealthily crawled into bed next to her without waking her up. Sleep evaded him, as his mind raced for a couple of hours before exhaustion took over.

Shining through the bedroom windows, the sun felt warm on her face. Mia slowly awoke and stretched, ready to begin the day. She looked over at Greg, who was still sound asleep. Usually he was up before her, but she thought she'd go ahead and get coffee and breakfast going. She headed downstairs and noticed when she got to the living room that the book Greg had brought home was open. When they went to bed, she was certain that they had shut it. She walked over to it and was about to shut it again when she noticed their names had been added to it. She knew their names were not there last night. That's something that they definitely needed to discuss when Greg got up.

Soon, breakfast was on the table, and the coffee was poured. She figured she would yell at Greg to see if she could get him to wake up.

"Breakfast is ready!"

She waited a moment and didn't hear anything. She texted him, too. Maybe he was on his phone or in the bathroom. Then she padded back to the table and sat down to drink her coffee and eat her breakfast while she watched TV.

Greg woke up with a start. He looked around and realized that Mia was already up; maybe that was the noise he heard from the kitchen, he thought. He rushed downstairs.

"Morning! You made breakfast, thank you." Leaning over, he kissed Mia as he took a seat at the table. "How did you sleep?"

"Surprisingly well. You?"

"Struggled for a while, but I finally slept a little. Sorry I didn't get up to make you coffee." He looked exhausted and disheveled.

"Oh, please. I'm capable, don't worry about it." She forced a smile. She noticed something on his neck that wasn't there last night.

"What is that on your neck?" Mia asked.

"Oh, it's a shaving cut."

"You didn't shave this morning, Greg" She looked at him suspiciously. "Our names were added to the book. How in the hell is that possible, and what the hell did *we* do to get on that list?"

"Okay, hear me out. Last night I heard noises, so I came downstairs. There was a man in our living room. He said we have to agree to help him, and then he would remove our names from the list. He said he would be in touch."

"Are you serious?" Mia then sat there with her mouth open. All the color drained from her face.

"Yeah, can you believe that bullshit? He looks familiar to me and I just can't put my finger on why."

"Why didn't you wake me up or call the police?"

"I didn't want you to worry, I'm sorry."

Glaring at Greg, Mia said, "We'll talk about this later." Mia was short with him, and wanted to really rip into him, but she knew she needed time to calm down. "Look, I'm sure this is all a big misunderstanding. Just take that book to work. Hopefully that weird guy will pick it up and we can forget about it."

"Something else happened last night. Don't freak out. After he left the house he had a dead body and these *things*, like ate the dead woman. I don't know what they all are, but Mia, I'm scared."

Mia's face softened and her jaw dropped. "What is going on around here?" She asked in a fearful tone. She was obviously near tears and needed to process what he had told her.

AS GREG PULLED UP IN FRONT OF MIA'S STORE, HE noticed something was amiss. The door didn't appear to be secure, and he was distraught. He cautiously opened the door. Peering inside, he saw Santa standing in the shadows. Greg could smell the cigar he was smoking.

"Ah, good, you brought my book back. Greg that

wasn't something you were supposed to witness, last night. But that's a necessary evil, so to speak." Santa was annoyed with Greg for the simple fact that he was alive.

Greg appeared perplexed. "Look, here's your book back. Just leave us alone."

"Greg, I depend on blood to survive. We need an isolated location to feast and you and Mia are going to help with that. I'll see you at your cabin late tonight."

"Please just go, *please*. I have to plan for our cabin in the woods, Christmas vacation. I just don't have time for this. " Greg attempted to plead with him.

"Invite some friends on your trip, but not ones that you'll miss much. I'll handle it from there."

"Fine. I'll invite some friends. Will four be enough for you?"

"It'll do. See you later tonight, when you least expect it." As Santa was leaving with his "naughty list" book, Greg recoiled, but was grateful he was gone.

Greg picked up the phone to invite his friends out to the cabin for the holidays.

"Hey Matt, yeah, it's been a while. Mia and I were wondering if you and Angie would like to head out to our cabin tonight for the holidays, since you guys normally spend Christmas alone?"

"Hi Greg. Nice to hear from you. Should be fun. I'll

run it by Angie, but I'm sure she's down. We will meet you out there by 6 pm. Sounds good to you?"

"Perfect, thanks man, looking forward to it." Greg hung up and dialed another friend, Marcus.

"Hey Marcus! It's been too long. Last-minute invite, but are you and Melinda interested in meeting us at the cabin with Matt and Angie? We thought it'd be fun to have a low key, fun, couple's Christmas."

"Hey man, that sounds great. We will meet you there, looking forward to it! We decided to stay home this year, but that sounds like a better plan. I'll talk to the wife, but it should be fine." Marcus replied. Both hung up and Marcus seemed excited for the trip.

Greg made the calls, hoping it would be enough people to appease Santa. He also was terrified it wouldn't be. He should call Mia to give her a heads up about the change. She would probably want to pack nicer clothes now and run to the store to get more groceries.

"Hey babe, guess what? Matt, Angie, Marcus, and Melinda are going to meet us at the cabin tonight. Sounds fun, huh?"

"Sure. Was this at the insistence of a Santa, perhaps?"

"Um, well yeah, but it'll be more fun with friends. I'm sure it's nothing to worry about."

"Fine. I'll run to the store and grab more food to pack in the ice chest. See you in a couple of hours. We should leave earlier now to get the cabin ready since we will have guests."

Mia clicked off her cell and grabbed her keys and clutch and headed out. As she was about to get in her car, she saw a scraggly-looking santa smoking across the street. He was boring holes in her with a focused stare. With a flick of his cigar, he continued to stare at Mia. He sauntered over to her. She couldn't help but feel drawn to him in a perverse way, but she was frozen in equal parts both fear and desire. He invaded her personal space with his rancid breath. The spell was broken, and Mia was grateful.

"Who are you, and what do you want?" Mia held his gaze with admirable confidence.

"I'm Santa, I thought Greg told you about me. He certainly didn't tell me how beautiful you are, though."

Mia scoffed. "Huh, well he doesn't always see me that way. Look, I've got some shopping to do. Greg is doing what you have asked. You don't need me for anything."

"That's not true." Moving closer to Mia, he whispered in her ear, "I need a Mrs. Claus. Are you interested?"

Laughing, Mia says, "You have amnesia? Remember Greg? You might be better served finding someone single." She shook her head.

Santa grabbed Mia and pulled her close. They were hidden from prying eyes. He kissed her neck and bit her sensuously and sucked the blood that flowed. She tried to push away from him, but he was too strong. When he was done, his eyes burned dark as night and he knew his future would be with Mia.

She shivered as goose pimples covered her flesh, and she felt nauseous and light headed. She leaned against her SUV.

"See you soon." Santa sneered and walked away.

When Mia looked up, he was already gone. She grabbed a kleenex from her bag and blotted the blood that remained dripping down her neck.

She quickly got in her car and sped off as fast as she could, since she was now running late. She could feel him trying to finagle his way into her soul. Which was impossible. Such a strange thought, but she couldn't quite shake it. As she pulled into the grocery store, she shook her head, cleared her throat, and strode inside like she owned the place, in typical Mia fashion.

GREG BROUGHT ALL THE BAGS DOWNSTAIRS AND put them by the front door. He left work pretty early as Mia had suggested. Looking at his watch, it looked like they should leave about 1:00 pm, which would have them arrive at their Grand Lake cabin about 3:00 pm. He had the ice chest ready and he opened the door and carried it to their SUV. He grabbed the suitcases and finished loading everything in record time. As he closed the trunk, he turned; there was Santa, in uncomfortable proximity. He blew smoke in his face and Greg coughed while Santa began laughing eerily.

"See you around midnight at your cabin. You better hope that your friends show up, or you'll face the same horror as they will. I'll have friends with me too, by the way." Santa started to walk away. He turned back to Greg and said, "Hey Greg, your wife is hot. Keep an eye on her." He laughed all the way down the driveway and disappeared around the corner. Greg ran after him, but when he turned the corner, there was no sign of Santa. He walked back up to the car just as Mia was coming outside.

"What are you doing?"

"Santa was here and he just vanished. He's just creepy as fuck, and I want him to go away."

"Hopefully after tonight, he will be gone and we will never have to see him again. The bags are loaded. I think we have everything. Are you ready?"

"Yep, let's go." They both got into the SUV. Greg was driving, and Mia read as they headed to the mountains.

The tension was palpable for the next two hours on the way to their cabin.

LODGEPOLE PINES STOOD TALL AND DENSE NEAR the cabin deep in the Rocky Mountains. Snow plows would soon no longer be clearing the roads, because of the next impending storm. The drifts were already several feet tall from last night. In front of the cabin, the snow was unblemished and sparkled like the stars in the Colorado skies. Denver had only had flurries for the last few days, so this was a surprise, as they'd forgotten to check the weather. Greg texted Matt and Marcus to leave as soon as they could because of the inclement weather. They responded quickly with how they had already left and would be there in an hour.

Spending Christmas with their friends should be something to look forward to, but it felt ominous with the impending snow storm combined with the expected yet unwanted visit from Santa. As they pulled up to the front of the modern rustic cabin, their excitement was waning.

Mia freshened up the cabin while Greg got the bags from their new Bronco that Mia demanded. Greg knew this was her baby, so he was careful when loading and unloading anything. He didn't want to piss her off.

As Mia was cleaning the cabin, she still hoped for a bit of romance this weekend and the openness from Greg to connect on a level they hadn't yet; agreement on having children. She hummed as she added the special touches to the two guest rooms, including small bowls of chocolates, and she almost forgot her encounter with Santa earlier. They'd just built this cabin a couple of years ago on the small lake, but it was a natural made one that was stunning. Looking around the cabin, she realized how much she loved it here and wanted to live here after they sold the toy store and retired.

"Honey, is everything out of the car?" Mia yelled out of one of the guest rooms. She really didn't want to go back outside, as it was dusk, the air was frigid, and the skies were darkening to the west.

"Yep, I got everything. We're good." Greg said with trepidation. He felt on edge, considering how the evening would probably go and his encroaching guilt.

He had been looking forward to relaxing and getting away from all the craziness of his mundane daily life and enjoying at least a brief respite. Now, with the unexpected events that he was potentially facing, relaxing was likely out of the question. Gazing out of the wall of windows facing the trees, he looked up at the trees that held shadows and secrets while the darkened skies were inching closer. Greg shuddered in the cold that seeped into his bones, even though the cabin was warm. He hoped they wouldn't be here longer than expected. After Greg got the fireplace going and turned on the Christmas tree lights that decorated a beautiful fake Douglas fir they had put up a few weeks ago, he and Mia snuggled up with each other and set out a bottle of red wine to share. Greg poured the wine and proposed a toast.

"May this respite be over soon!" Greg said.

"Cheers." Mia clinked her wine glass against his, and they drank.

Greg leaned in to kiss Mia and noticed her neck. He knew what it was from without even asking. Mia glanced up and realized that he saw it and without thinking, she caressed the injury.

Knocking could be heard at the door. Greg got up, walked over, and opened it wide to see his friends had arrived together. "Hey guys! It's great you made it before the storm got worse. You ride together?" Greg asked with curiosity, he was surprised since he didn't think they knew each other that well.

"We have been hanging out a lot the last several months, so I offered to drive, since I knew where the cabin was," Matt said as he walked in with he and Angie's bags. Marcus and Melinda followed.

"Hi everyone!" Mia got up to give everyone hugs. "Hey Greg, grab a couple more bottles of wine."

Greg did what Mia asked and also grabbed a few beers for the guys. By the time he got to the huge sectional in the living room, everyone was getting reacquainted and laughing. His friends appeared comfortable, so Greg relaxed. He put on a Christmas playlist that was festive with a mix of modern Christmas songs and some classics that most people loved. They had prepared a wonderful Christmas Eve spread of heavy hors d'oeuvres buffet style in the kitchen for everyone to enjoy as they drank their wine and beer. Everyone seemed to enjoy themselves. The ambiance was perfect. After a couple of hours passed, the conversation lulled, and everyone looked exhausted.

The wind picked up outside and howled like an ancient beast coming to life. Everyone looked at each other, then out towards the wall of windows facing the forest at the back of the cabin. Snow had fallen again, with delicate flakes drifting to the ground below. Mia rose and went to the frosted glass to admire the beautiful forest and falling snow. In the recesses of the trees, she saw what she thought was a shadowy human form.

"Hey Greg, come here."

"What is it?" Greg joined Mia at the windows.

"I think I saw someone near the trees back there, I—"

She pointed to the area where she had seen the shadowy form.

"I don't see anything. Are you sure? Maybe it's just the darkness playing tricks on you."

"Greg, I'm sure."

"Well, it looks like they're gone now, " he said, then looked back at the coffee table. "Whew. We really polished off that wine. It's been a long day, and I think I'm going to head for bed. Care to join?" Mia nodded her head yes in agreement.

"Hey everyone, we are going to turn in. Does anyone need anything? Oh, there are bottles of water in the refrigerator and everyone should have a fan in your room in case you sleep hot or need white noise. It was a blast. Thanks everyone, we will cook you guys a big breakfast in the morning. Night all." Greg said jovially, then took Mia by the hand and went to their bedroom.

Everyone said their goodnights and turned into their respective bedrooms. Mia changed into cozy clothes but found herself drawn to the window again, this time in the bedroom, just looking out. A shadow was out there, something that stood out from other dark recesses in the woods, and it seemed to stare back at her just as she stared at it. It looked human, yet not. Bloodthirsty mutants, ghostly, gray, and shadowy in form, awaited their chance to kill. It opened its mouth wider than nature intended, and let out a scream that sounded like tires screeching at the drag races.

In reflex, Mia screamed too.

Greg ran in from the bathroom, looking at Mia with confusion. He saw something climb up to the cabin's roof near the window and then understood Mia's reaction and her words earlier; he should have believed her. Securing the front door and the windows alike made Mia feel safer. Greg hoped it was enough.

"I locked up everything already. We should be good." Greg didn't believe his own words, any more than Mia did.

The fireplace was roaring with life, providing a false sense of safety. Wishing it was Santa's reindeer on the roof instead of what he knew was up there, the noises persisted. Each growing moment felt like an eternity as the sounds vibrated throughout the cabin. More than one shadow creature was now on the roof. Their friends had joined them in the living room after hearing all the commotion. Mia and Greg did not know how they all would survive this Christmas Eve night with the unholy Santa outside, joined by his shadow creatures. Immense guilt took hold of Greg, as no one knew what was promised. The devil was here to collect, and he couldn't stop the chain of events from happening.

GREG AND MIA HELD EACH OTHER IN FRONT OF the fire, since the power went out exactly at midnight. Greg wasn't sure how they could protect themselves, a gun didn't seem like it would kill the things outside. Even worse was the silence that had come with the shadows. Sounds of winter like wind, owls, and wolves were absent; there was nothing.

"Mia, I'm going to check the doors to make sure nothing is trying to get in. Use the heated fireplace poker as a weapon if needed. It's the only thing we have."

"Please hurry back, Greg, I'm scared, we all are!"

Greg looked around at his wife and friends, then reluctantly went to the front door. He could hear the shadow creatures waiting patiently behind it as they were whispering about sacrificial lambs and Greg's reward—a promise of survival. Opening the door was a compulsion he couldn't resist. He couldn't stop himself, even though his brain was screaming not to. The driving compulsion forced his body forward. He wanted to tell Mia and his friends to run, but stepped aside so the evil could enter. They promised him it would be quick.

He was about to yell out at Mia so she could get away,

but they turned to him instead. They pulled and tore at Greg, shredding him like a cooked chicken. The shadow creatures were competing for the meat and didn't want to share. Greg was being cannibalized and devoured by greedy creatures that behaved like they had consumed nothing other than woodland animals, and this was a celebration for the evil inside the cabin, which then moved to the living room.

The front door that was already open, was all the invitation Santa needed. He looked more evil with the darkness to his back, gnarly, long, thick nails, and gnashing teeth ready to kill. A Santa hat sat atop his long, flowing white hair and his long beard caught snowflakes in it while he puffed on a blazing cigar. On either side, two shadow creatures eagerly joined Santa to continue their Christmas Eve feast. The snow storm continued to rage outside, and through the doorway everyone could see and hear another shadow creature and a reindeer that sneered; its eyes were a black soulless amalgamation of everything unholy and blasphemous.

Santa unleashed his shadow creatures, and hell ensued in the living room. The backdrop of the Christmas tree and comforting fire juxtaposed the shadow creatures attacking Marcus and Matt. They tackled them and knocked them over and tore into them like a pack of wolves. Once they were done, they leered at the three women.

"Wait. Ladies, come here. Since Greg promised me your lives, and he accidentally got himself devoured by my creatures, only one of you needs to sacrifice yourself for the greater good of keeping my creatures happy. Actually Mia, since Greg is no longer here, you will be mine now. In the meantime, the remaining two of you have five minutes to decide or I'll choose for you."

Angie and Melinda looked at each other, terrified. Angie broke out into a run for the door. She grabbed their car keys and tried to get past the snow drifts and the reindeer, but the reindeer moved more quickly than Angie thought it could, pushing her face down in the snow. It was ripping her sweater and chewing her clothes off with an enormous chunk of flesh from her back. She screamed out in great pain and fear.

"*Get her.*" Santa said to his shadow creatures. They bolted towards Angie and she screamed again when they reached her as she was still being held down by the reindeer, blood was seeping into the snow from where her back had been ripped, she didn't stand a chance. The creatures started on her sides and worked out the organs, then ripped her sinewy flesh on each side. They devoured her until her head, bones, and feet were the only things that remained alongside the blood that covered much of the snow near the open door.

Santa opened up the naughty list and showed it to Mia.

"Look Mia, yours and Greg's names are disappearing." The ink of their names slowly and methodically lifted, swirled above the book, and then dissipated.

Melinda and Mia looked at Santa with a primal fear embedded in their soul. They knew there was no escaping their fate of becoming food for creatures that were of a higher pecking order. They were otherworldly, and they could only hope that they would leave after getting what they wanted.

"Santa, Greg thought he knew you. Did you know him?" Mia asked.

"Yes, we went to school together. My name was Steve. He saw my name on the naughty list because of this. You know, what happened to you tonight, happened to me. I'll explain it further when you join me. Mia, we will rule together and this is what *every* Christmas Eve can look like for you. Enticing, yes? Eternal life with me and my new family. What more could you ask for?" He asked, knowing the answer to his question. He moved close to Mia and stood firmly in front of her. He lightly raked his long nails down her face and lingered on her lips. With a sensual gaze, he then kissed her as passionately as he could, knowing he'd see her soon. "Let's go," he spoke to his creatures and his reindeer. "Merry Fucking Christmas ladies!" He slammed the door shut after they left. Small mounds of snow were inside near the door, and the women shivered while hugging each other for warmth and comfort. Mia held back the desire to vomit. They both broke down and sobbed. After a while, their crying subsided, and they gained a minimal amount of composure. On the kitchen table, Steve had left the naughty list book. It was closed, but then suddenly opened and flipped to the last names of Bender. Melinda saw her name appear in a beautiful golden font that quickly turned into a black ancient one that looked like it had been there for decades. They looked at each other with complete horror.

Both spoke in unison, "Fuck."

PART FOUR
SPRING

APOLOGETIC ANNA

usk approached and Abby focused on swimming near the dock, oblivious to the upcoming nightfall and the dangers surrounding it. The humidity was suffocating, making the swim more necessity than pleasure. Crickets chirped and cicadas could be heard at a deafening level, unaware of the looming depravity. Abby loved to swim at night to clear her head, and tonight was no different. Normally Levi would join her, but he had to finish a few things at his parent's house; he had to skip the swim with Abby, promising to join her later.

Spring Break was nearly over as her thoughts kept wandering back to Levi, currently at his nearby lake house. Every spring and summer, she looked forward to the two weeks out of the year they spent together. Their parents went to college together and remained the best of friends all these years later. Yesterday she saw Levi for the first time in a new way, and those intrusive thoughts were welcomed with a sigh of longing. She thought about him nearly every waking moment and had such high hopes for more than a great friendship.

As Abby pulled herself up from the water onto the rotted wooden section of the dock, she noticed something glimmering from the sun's reflection at the edge of the woods. Toweling off and lying her beach towel by the firepit that was blazing, she sauntered over to get a closer look. Walking on the worn path to where the buried item lay beneath leaves and brush, she hesitated to pick it up. Old and battered, the doll caked with grime and wearing a tattered dress gave clues to being lost for decades. Deciding to throw caution to the wind, she wiped off as much dirt and leaves from it that would fall away using her bare hands. She carried it back to the dock and set it down on one of the Adirondack chairs as she draped the towel around her shoulders and tempered the fire. She looked at the tag on the inside of the dolls' dress and scribbled in faded ink, the name Anna was clear.

Abby sat down and grabbed a beer from the ice chest. She looked at the beer she accidentally picked up. Stella Artois wouldn't do. That was for Levi. She wrinkled her nose and put the beer back, digging for something better. Finding a few mini bottles of Skrewball, she sat back, satisfied with her choice.

Stella Artois tastes like piss. I don't understand why Levi loves it, she thought.

Waiting on Levi to arrive, she chugged the first bottle of whiskey and started her second as she daydreamed of what she hoped would happen between them. Interrupted by someone yelling her name, she snapped out of it. Branches cracking and heavy footfalls could be heard behind her. Turning around, she saw Levi with his sexy lopsided grin.

"Abby! There you are. I've been looking for you." Levi walked up, grabbed a beer and sat in the chair next to her. Holding her gaze, he asked, "What the hell is that in the other chair?" Pointing towards the doll, he chugged his Stella and waited for an answer.

"Excuse me sir, it's a vintage doll that I dragged over here from the woods." Spoken in her most fake snobbish tone, she glanced over at him and gave him the most flirtatious smile she could manage.

"We had plans to meet here. Did you forget or did you have more chores at home to do?" Abby asked.

She knew he could see her dock from his lake house, they were actually neighbors. Abby studied him like a textbook. Lost in thought again, she didn't see Levi stand up and move toward her, setting his beer bottle down. He stood before her with eyes that screamed with desire. He gently grabbed her hands, encouraging her to stand up. They stood facing each other at a comfortable, close distance.

"Abby, I have to be honest with you. This trip, um, I looked forward to seeing you more than ever before. I really care about you. We've known each other for so long and have been great friends. I want to be more, but I need to know what you are feeling? I don't want to be wrong about this. That would be awkward." He laughed nervously.

Abby looked at Levi and melted. She moved her body closer to his, and there was no air able to escape between them. Abby was still in her bikini from her swim earlier, but the heat was not only rising from the fire pit, but deep within her. Levi's desire was apparent as he gently kissed her mouth slowly, skimmed her breasts, and he gave her bottom a light squeeze. He broke their passionate embrace to throw her towel down on the dock by the fire and they kissed again, but with more force and aggression. Abby untied her bikini top, and it fell to her side. With care, Levi removed the other half of her bikini and tossed it behind him. While frantically kissing, they explored each other's bodies.

AFTERWARDS, THE COMFORTABLE SILENCE between them felt natural as they held each other tight, with lingering, light caresses. They began to hungrily kiss and caress each other again, but they knew they would have to get dressed soon, as their parents would be home anytime. Their parents were close friends and went out for drinks. A local bar, *Sutures,* is where the two families spent much of their time. Being in their twenties now, it wouldn't be the end of the world if their parents caught them together, but it wouldn't be ideal either.

"Levi, does this mean we're dating?" She gazed into his eyes, but was nervous about his answer. She brushed her chestnut hair away from her perfectly shaped lips. Her head was buzzing with excitement and bourbon, thinking of the possibilities. But self doubt was creeping in as it often does.

"Abby, I would love nothing more than to be exclusive.

We graduate from college soon and we wouldn't have to date long distance for long; maybe for two to three months? We've known each other for years. I love you, and there isn't anyone I would ever want in this world but you."

Continuing to lay next to each other, each lost in thought for a few moments, the sounds of nature were enveloped in a sudden silence.

"Levi, I–I don't know what to say. Well, yes, I do. I have always loved you. I mean, before, it was as a friend, but now it's definitely more. She laughed and looked at Levi.

"Then we agree. Let's get dressed, and we can tell our parents the great news. They will be so excited to hear this. Let me grab your swimsuit." Levi gave her a sly smile.

He reached over to grab her bikini bottoms when he heard a small childlike voice behind him. He quickly turned as a small hand reached out, touching his own hand and holding Abby's bikini.

"Hi, I'm Anna. Who are you guys? Thanks for saving me from drowning in the mud and branches! Oh, here's your clothes...um you two might want to get dressed pretty quickly." Her voice and tone mimicked Abby's to a tee. As she handed Abby's bikini bottoms to Levi, he quickly grabbed them as his eyes widened in disbelief at what he was seeing, and the hair on his arms stood at attention.

"Fuck! What the hell?" Levi pulled his hand away and saw that there was a thin jagged gash with blood pooling at his feet. He grabbed his shirt after he put his swim trunks back on to stop the bleeding.

"Oh, no. I did it again. I'm so sorry. I try so hard to be good, but I just...can't." Anna spoke softly.

She hobbled slowly towards Abby. Blonde, dirty hair, partially covered her eyes, which moved rapidly back and forth with a quiet clicking.

"My God, what are you? You look like a ventriloquist doll that crawled up from Hell." Abby spoke with trepidation and fear melting into sheer horror.

"Goodness no, silly." Laughing, she crept even closer to Abby.

"I have a passive aggressive personality, but I haven't been to Hell yet." With a permanent plastic smile plastered across her face, Anna laughed again. "You are so funny, Abby! I like you, but stop backing away from me. I want to *play*. My brother over there wants to play too. He's not as nice as I am, though."

Looking toward the wooded area in the recesses of the trees, a ghostly figure could be seen. Abby grabbed Levi, and they ran to Abby's lake house.

LEVI HIT ONE OF THE ROCKING CHAIRS ON THE porch looking back out where the skyline met the water. He looked over toward the other rocking chair where the doll was already sitting. Her head squeaked and turned to look at Levi. She pointed her little arm out towards the yard and the woods beyond. The ghostly image appeared to float at a snail's pace, getting closer and closer.

He heard the front door open, and he saw it slam shut. He stood up and decided he would go in and check on Abby since he had stupidly zoned out. The blood moon shone brightly behind him and silhouetted the ghostly figure he didn't see approaching.

"Abby?"

He waited, yet his call was met with silence. A loud thump upstairs caused him to jump.

"Abby?" Levi yelled out again.

No response came from Abby. He felt a rising sense of dread as he knew he should go upstairs and face whatever fate would behold him there. Fear held him back. Trying to move forward- he knew Abby needed him- but some unseen force continued to prevent him from reaching the stairs. The air became thick and Levi began to shiver as the cold hit him abruptly while his breath could be seen in front of him.

What the fuck, he thought. "I'm coming!" Levi yelled.

As Levi cautiously walked up the stairs, out of the corner of his eye, he saw a mini razor come toward his ankle.As he reached down and touched it, touching himself, he looked at the blood dripping from his hand.

"What the f–"

He dodged the succession of additional attempted cuts and rushed upstairs to get Abby.

"Levi, I know what this looks like, but I didn't do this!"

Abby was sitting on her bed with a steady stream of blood trickling from her right arm with an increased numbing sensation creeping up and shock seeping into her unavoidable consciousness.

"I know. It's that fucking demon doll. Something weird and unexplainable is happening. We need to get out of here. Can you stand? Abby?"

Levi's eyes locked onto Abby, waiting for her to respond. He needed her to say something now more than ever. However, Abby simply slouched, and slumped to the side of her bed, as her eyes drifted to a close.

Shaking Abby gently, he yelled, "Hey wake up! We have to get out of here! Abby, please." He pleaded with desperation and terror.

Abby stirred slightly, weakened by the loss of blood. Levi observed the crimson stains on her thighs, the white comforter doing its best to soak up the blood that continued to spill and flow.

"Abby! Come on, let's go. We can't stay here. We won't make it."

He grabbed her from her armpits to help her stand. Abby mumbled something incoherent as her head lolled. Raising her head and opening her eyes appeared to be a monumental feat. Levi finally gained some footing and helped Abby off of the blood-soaked bed. They moved cautiously towards the top of the stairs and deliberately stepped down slowly to ease the pain of Abby's injuries. Grabbing the car keys from the end table by the door, they stepped outside onto the porch. As they moved toward the car, one of the rocking chairs creaked as it rocked back and forth in quick movements. The doll jumped down. In its little hand sat a small razor with specks of dried blood. Anna moved her arm quickly and the rocking chair and everything in its path cleared like they were being thrown by an invisible malevolent force. The doll moved from in front of the chair in an unnatural and jerky manner. It raised its arm again with the razor blade coming toward them.

"I'm so sorry. I didn't mean to cut you both so deep. Please forgive me." The doll spoke to them as if they have been lifelong friends. "Sometimes I just need to cause a little pain. It's what I was *told* to do. My name is Anna. Oh, wait, I told you that already. I wouldn't step off the porch if I were you. Turn around." Anna motioned for them to look at the yard. There stood a boy that looked unnaturally pale, yet had a slight sparkle. His soulless eyes were staring through Abby and Levi.

"Levi, what is going on?" Abby whimpered.

"I wish I knew," he whispered.

"See? That's why you shouldn't leave just yet. We should watch a movie together! It'll be so fun!" Anna was excited to have friends again. It's been decades since she'd had any attention.

Anna moved behind them to get them to go inside. "Come on you two, we don't have all night! I mean, I wish we did, but my brother looks pretty upset and you probably don't have long until..."

"Until what Anna? Just tell us."

"Um, no thank you. Do you have the movie *Scream*? It's so good! Don't you think so Abby?"

Abby looked at the talking doll with a blank stare. Anna hobbled over and stood in front of her.

"Oh Abby, come on, snap out of it." Anna said as she cut her on her right leg behind her knee.

"Oh gosh, I did it again! Abby, I'm so sorry. My

brother told me too." Anna stared up at Abby, expecting her to say something.

Levi went to find *Scream* on one of the streaming services, hoping to distract Anna. He lucked out and found it, and promptly started the movie.

"Hey Anna, *Scream* is on for you. Why don't you come in the living room and watch it with us, you know, like you wanted."

Anna ambled her short stubby doll legs over to the couch in front of the television. She awkwardly hopped up onto the couch and seemed to be mesmerized by the TV. Levi and Abby gave each other knowing looks and backed up near the front door.

Suddenly, knocking could be heard at the front door. It rose in volume and frequency. Levi peeked out of the window and saw nothing. He shrugged and walked back to the living room to sit with Abby who joined Anna again, who didn't notice her previous attempt to leave. Anna caused an uncomfortable feeling of dread. They watched *Scream* in silence. Aggressive knocking began again. It was evident that whatever it was wanted in, but needed an invitation.

Levi got up again and approached the front door, but he hesitated with his hand around the door knob. Shaking, he opened the door with quiet panic. Standing in the doorway was a young male ghostly figure that nearly sparkled from the moonlight behind him, but this time they could see him. Evil intent oozed from his sinister smile.

The ghost and Anna were quickly upon Levi with Anna's razor providing unwanted and frequent deep cuts. The ghost held Levi in place by an unseen force. Abby was distraught, as there was nothing she could do. Tears continued to stream down Abby's face as she tried to wipe them away, but her trembling hand was unable to keep up with the flood.

"Anna, can I go now? You two got what you wanted. You don't need both of us."

"Not quite. I need to get out of this doll, Abby," hissing her response.

"Tony, hold her down." Anna said. The ghostly boy moved swiftly and held Abby in place by standing on her. Abby didn't understand how he could keep her in place since she didn't feel the brunt of his weight. Confusion and fear intertwined deep into her soul. Abby wanted everything to be over; she couldn't fathom surviving this night. Anna, next to Abby, raised her arms and began chanting in an all too familiar voice. It quickly made Abby feel sick to her stomach. While lightning outside lit up the shadows in the home, a silhouette in human form stood next to Anna, silently watching them both.

As no one was watching Levi, he crept closer to Abby

and slammed a crystal vase on the back of the doll's head, knocking her down. He brought the vase down on her head repeatedly, screaming louder each time. Anna's head laid in pieces on the floor next to her decapitated body. Levi took the razor blade from the doll's hand, shoving it deep inside his pocket. He stood up and looked at Abby. The ghostly boy had disappeared, but the ghostly woman that was contained in the doll Anna remained, looking on.

Abby and Levi scrambled to abruptly leave for a second time. The new ghostly woman cackled as they left. She would follow them outside and follow them forever.

GHOSTLY FEARS:
APOLOGETIC ANNA II

As Levi and Abby ran toward Levi's lake house, they couldn't shake the feeling that they were being watched. Stopping in the front yard of Levi's home, he checked his front pockets for his keys. The khaki cargo shorts had deep pockets, so it took an extra few seconds to fish out the car keys. Abby brushed her hair away from her face as she looked behind them nervously and shivered when she noticed the ghostly figure in the shadows of the grove of trees that hovered closely to the lake. Darkness had settled, and evil waited patiently.

"Abby, let's go!" Levi yelled at Abby.

She turned quickly, grabbing Levi's hand with a firm grip. They ran quickly to Levi's car.

Reaching Levi's gray Charger, he unlocked the doors with his fob, and they rushed inside. Starting the car and backing out of the drive, he caught a glimpse of the ghost of Anna watching them. She lifted her right arm up and opened her mouth wide. Before Levi could see what happened next, he quickly drove away.

DRIVING CAUTIOUSLY THROUGH THE WINDING rural roads of the lake house community proved to be difficult in the sudden torrential downpour. Levi glanced in the rearview mirror and noticed a ghastly woman in the backseat. She was an apparition of sorts and looked vaguely familiar. He let out an audible gasp and looked at Abby. He looked back in the mirror and the woman was gone.

"What the fuck! Abby, look in the backseat, tell me what you see?"

Abby turned around to see what Levi saw, but she saw nothing.

"You okay? You seem on edge and a bit scared."

Abby waited for him to respond. She reassured him by rubbing his leg and gave him a thigh squeeze and a moment to think.

"The ghost that came out of that fucking doll at your lake house, I saw her in the backseat. She is following us. She's attached herself to us!" Levi spoke in a loud whisper.

He cut his eyes at Abby to check her reaction. Abby tensed up and looked back again. She still didn't see anything. They sat in an uncomfortable silence for a few moments during the drive home. Watching the rain hit the windshield, Abby traced the falling raindrops on the window as they fell. She appeared lost in her thoughts and struggled with what to say to him.

"Levi, I don't see anything. Are you sure it's not just your mind playing tricks on you?"

"Abby, are you serious? After everything we *just* went through, you have to ask me that? You've got to be kidding. *I know what I saw.*"

Rolling his eyes and tightening his grip on the

steering wheel, he closed his mouth and gritted his teeth. He didn't want to say anything that he would regret. He focused on the road ahead so he could get Abby home safely.

As they approached Abby's parent's home only an hour away from the lake, they both began to relax a bit. Levi began to think that maybe he imagined the ghost briefly riding in the backseat after all. He reached for Abby's hand, and held it firmly. She looked over at him and leaned in to give him a peck on the cheek. They locked eyes for a second and as Abby looked away, she suddenly saw that the ghost was back. Only this time, they both saw her.

Swerving the Charger to avoid another car close to an exit ramp, Levi slammed the brakes and spun out. Abby was quick to scream and braced for impact. Fortunately, they didn't hit another car, but there was a guardrail adjacent to the passenger side. Levi put the hazard lights on and got out to look at the damage. The Charger was mere inches away from the guardrail and didn't appear to have any scratches on it. He ran his hands through his hair and let out a long sigh of relief. He gave Abby a thumbs-up as she gazed at him through the window.

Her heart felt like it was going to jump out of her chest. Abby couldn't get over the fact that he had turned into such a good-looking guy. She never in a million years when they were kids, ever thought that they would end up together. His rugged good looks and bright blue eyes could now melt her heart a hundred times over. Her thoughts were alternating between what just happened and thoughts of her feelings for Levi. They simply couldn't die after finally realizing what they meant to each other. Meanwhile, Levi walked back to the driver's side and quickly got in the car.

"Well, at least there isn't any body or paint damage to the car. I'll have to take it in to have the tires and axles looked at. Abby, you okay? I'm so sorry about that, but do you believe that I saw her now?"

Abby nodded her head yes with wide, scared eyes, despite her earlier thoughts about Levi.

"The ghost and the car basically nearly made my heart stop!" She kept looking toward the backseat, expecting to see the ghost again.

Levi started the car up and waited for the traffic to clear. "Let's just hope that we get to your house without anything else happening. I don't think my heart can take anymore of this."

Hitting the gas and merging back on the highway, they were only minutes away from where Abby lives with her parents when she isn't away at college. The minutes felt like forever while Abby watched as everything sped by the window. She thought about the insanely large billboards that are meant to draw in the drivers and riders of the people traveling in the community mentioned in *Fahrenheit 451*. Most people in high school didn't appreciate it, but she loved Bradbury's style, especially *Something Wicked This Way Comes*. If only Levi had the same appreciation for literature. She sighed.

"You okay over there?" Levi asked.

"Huh? Oh yeah. I was thinking about books."

"Typical Abby." He grinned broadly at her for a moment, as they pulled into the driveway of Abby's sprawling house before them.

ABBY'S PARENTS WERE IN FINANCE AND REAL estate, and had done well for themselves.

The circle drive in front of their three-story white brick home with 10,000 square feet to boot, was beautiful with its wall of windows, pillars on either side of the double dark wood front doors, and embellished lion head door knockers. Manicured lawn and shrubbery were all the same size and style. Dwarf Burning Bush hedges lined the front wall of windows, providing a stark contrast of the white of the home and the red of the bushes. The understated water fountain out front in the center of the circular drive was surrounded by simple small Boxwoods. There wasn't a fence or a gate since it sits back from the road and wasn't visible from the street when people were driving by. They have a state-of-the-art security system and an officer friend that patrols regularly, so they have always felt safe here.

"Every time I'm here I can't believe how damn huge this house is." Levi said, laughing as they got out of his car.

Abby smiled. "Honestly, I feel the same. My parents don't act like they have money, they're grateful for what they have. They didn't grow up with money, so it's nice that they are casual and fun most of the time. We have some charity events that we have to go to, and they are formal, but it's fun to dress up occasionally. There's one coming up, it's a children's hospital benefit. Not sure if we are going now though, considering what's happening and all."

Levi locked his car and stuck his keys in his pocket. They left in a rush and didn't take anything with them, so they held hands instead of grabbing luggage and headed toward the front door. There was a hidden keypad to get in the house if needed, and Abby punched in the code.

She pushed open one of the mahogany doors and stepped inside. Levi followed, closing the door and locking it.

"Hey, Abby, we should call our parents since we left in a rush. Do you have your cell phone?"

Abby felt around her pockets and realized she'd likely dropped it in their rush to get away.

"I don't have mine. You have yours?"

Levi shook his head no. "We can call them on the landline. You still have one, right?"

"Yeah, my parents refuse to get rid of it. I'm relieved that we have it now. I would always give them a hard time over it. Who knew the parents were right?"

Levi called his parents and told them what happened over the phone. Except he didn't, he lied. He made up an excuse that he had a friend going through a family emergency and rushed back to be with him, and Abby tagged along. They didn't feel like driving back to the lake house, so they came to Abby's instead. He didn't want to tell them the truth over the phone, so he made up the story of his friend, and hoped they bought it. He asked them to tell Abby's parents too. They would pack up his and Abby's stuff and bring it with them when they came back in a couple of days.

"Why did you make up that bullshit story?"

"There is no fucking way I'm telling my parents about ghosts when they don't believe in ghosts to begin with.

Especially over the phone. I've thought about it, but I don't think we should tell them. At least not right now."

"Fine. I do think we need to tell them at some point though. They would have to believe us if both of us told them the same thing. We can talk more about that later after we eat dinner. I need a shower and a nap. Then we can grab something to eat, or DoorDash sounds perfect. Think about what you want."

Abby walked toward the stairs. Halfway up, she turned back toward Levi.

"Hey, I love you." She gave him a million-dollar smile, turned, and continued up the stairs.

Levi yelled after her, "I love you back!"

HE DECIDED HE DIDN'T WANT TO BE ALONE AND took the stairs two at a time until he reached the landing and walked to Abby's bedroom. She was already in the shower. He thought about joining her, but figured she probably needed her space. She's fiercely independent and loves time alone. He'd jump in the shower after she was done.

Abby came out of her bathroom wrapped in a towel

and went directly to her walk-in closet, dropped her towel, and put on a t-shirt. She bent over to pick up the towel and quickly towel dried her hair. She felt eyes on her. She turned around and didn't see anything.

"Hey Levi?"

She thought he was still in her bedroom, but she didn't see him. She slowly opened her bathroom door and saw Levi staring at the mirror above the sink, and the terror in his eyes was evident. The hair on her arms raised and she turned behind her as the ghost that inhabited the doll Anna stood before her, staring intensely at her. Anna slowly raised her right arm, pointing ahead. Opening her mouth wide made it easier for the black ooze to escape and pool around her on the floor.

Abby screamed.

Levi snapped out of his trance and turned around to see Abby, and she ran to him. He embraced her and she looked at where the ghost previously stood, and the black ooze still remained.

"I guess napping is out of the question." Levi said.

Abby started to sob while Levi continued to hold her. She clutched his shirt tightly and buried her face in his chest. He put his arms around her and comforted her as best he could. After Abby regained her composure, she breathed deeply a few times before trying to speak.

Speaking softly, Abby said, "Sorry. I lost it there. This

is scary shit, and we need to talk to someone that can help us. I have an idea. I'll get dressed. We leave in five minutes."

"Well, okay. I'll stay here while you dress, just in case." Levi said.

Levi sat in Abby's reading chair by the window and waited for her to get dressed. It didn't take her long. She pulled on a pair of leggings and took off her t-shirt and added a sports bra and a loose sweater. She slipped on her Nike trainers, grabbed a hair tie and put her hair in a quick bun. She brushed her teeth fast and swished some water around and spit in the sink. She wiped her mouth on the hand towel. She had natural beauty, and it was effortless for her to look stunning. He was lost in thought, admiring her, when she started yelling at him.

"Levi! Hey! We need to *go*." Abby was irritated.

"Oh, sorry. Yeah, let's go." He seemed a bit embarrassed.

They both headed downstairs and out the front door.

They quickly got back into the car. Levi looked at Abby and asked, "Where we headed?"

"Go to St. Michael's. I know a priest there." Abby said nonchalantly.

"A priest? Seriously? What priest do *you* know?" Levi was skeptical.

Abby was short of temper and time. "Just go, please!"

"Geez, okay."

"He's someone I went to high school with. A friend. I think he could maybe steer us in the right direction at least." Abby said, with hope in her eyes.

"Oh, fair enough then. I know where the church is."

PULLING INTO THE CHURCH PARKING LOT, IT WAS already nearly eight o'clock; they were unsure if they'd even be able to get in. They got out of the car, Levi locked it, and they walked to the front of the church. The doors were locked, as they were afraid they would be.

"Well, so much for that idea."

Abby sat down on the steps of the Catholic church. Levi joined her, sitting down as well. They both were silent for a time and noticed someone walking up toward the church. A priest with a pizza box was headed straight for them.

Abby stood up and spoke first. "Marcum, hi! How've you been? It's so good to see you!"

She moved in to hug him, the best she could with the pizza box there in front of him. He seemed genuinely happy to see her.

"Abby! It's been too long, how are you and why are you sitting on the steps of my church?"

"We have something we need to talk about with you, if you can. I can DoorDash more pizza so we can eat together while we talk. We don't have our cell phones, but I can charge it to my account if you let me use your phone?"

"Whatever you need Abby. Let's get inside and we can start on this pizza, at least." Father Marcum opened the door for them first and then he followed, closing the door and locking it behind him. He led them to his office, and they sat down in his cramped space. Father Marcum opened the pizza box on his desk and encouraged the two of them to grab a slice. He handed Abby his cell phone so she could order more pizza to be delivered and pay for it. She handed the phone back to Marcum when she was finished so he could track when it would be delivered.

"What can I do for the two of you?"

Abby and Levi looked at each other and Abby nodded, indicating she would speak first. That has always been their way to communicate who would start a conversation. When they were kids playing at the lake, it was to defend whatever actions they took and bounced off each other to avoid getting in trouble. As adults, this was different.

"Marcum, we have a serious problem that we need your advice on." Abby said.

"Go on." Father Marcum encouraged her to continue.

"We had something terrible happen to us at the lake and it has followed us here."

Father Marcum looked confused, "I see. You mean literally, that something followed you home?"

Abby nodded her head yes. "We encountered some supernatural beings at the lake and one of them appeared to us here. It's clearly attached to us. We think we killed one of the ghosts, it was the brother of the ghost that followed us here. We think she wants revenge and maybe something else. At my house she let a ton of black ooze leak out of her mouth and then disappeared. I don't know what that means. Can you help us? How do we get rid of her?"

Father Marcum sat there, quietly thinking about what Abby said. He pushed himself back and stood up.

"I have to go grab the pizza from downstairs, stay here. Okay?"

Abby and Levi both nodded their heads in agreement. They waited for Father Marcum to come back with the extra pizza. They both were starving, evident by the rumble of their stomachs. They hadn't eaten today, with the exception of the pizza slice given to them.

The door opened and Father Marcum had the pizza,

as well as a few sodas. Setting everything down on his desk, he sat down again to continue the discussion.

Abby spoke first, "We were hoping you could bless my house and make it safe from any and all ghostly entities. Is that possible?"

Father nodded his head. "Yes, I can bless your home, Abby. Just don't ask me to perform an exorcism." He laughed.

Abby and Levi laughed along with him, albeit nervously.

"There is no possession, just an unwanted ghost. I guess it could be worse." Abby said.

Father Marcum spoke gently, "It can always be worse Abby. But I will do what I can to help you both. Have you thought about researching who the ghost was? Finding out what happened to her?"

Levi spoke up, "No, we hadn't thought of that. Maybe that would help in figuring out how to make her go away. Do you have a computer we can use?"

"Yes, of course. You can use mine." He stood up so Levi could sit at Father Marcum's computer.

Levi began searching for missing children in the Table Rock Lake area where they have lake houses. No missing children or mothers popped up in any articles that fit the description of the ghosts.

"Why don't you look for lake accidents, not missing people." Abby suggested.

"I love how your mind works." Levi looked up at her and smiled.

"I'm going to go grab some bottled water for you two. Be back in a few minutes." Father Malcum left.

Levi began to Google lake accidents. He scrolled through numerous articles and pages that mentioned drownings, boat accidents, firework injuries, but nothing seemed to fit. He sat back for a moment to think. He ran his hands through his hair as he often did when he was stressed.

"I think I have an idea of what to look up. I remember my parents talking about a fire they heard about when they were younger. I'll try to see if I can find anything about burn victims or fires around the lake." He plugged in more info on the computer in hopes of getting lucky.

"Hopefully something you find will help us soon." Abby said with hope.

"Here we are, you two."

Father Marcum set two water bottles down on his desk for them.

"Find anything yet?"

"Maybe. Abby, what year did you say your dad used to go to the lake when he was a teenager?" Levi asked.

"Oh, gosh, like the early 80s. Why?"

"Same for my dad. Did you know they were friends as teenagers? They've never mentioned it to me. You?"

"No, I thought they became friends as adults. What makes you think it was before that?"

"This."

Levi pointed to an article with two teen boys that were interviewed about a fire at the lake. It was Levi and Abby's dad's together in the photo. They had never seen this before and they were both stunned.

"What the hell? They knew each other during that fire?" Abby questioned.

"Not only that, they were asked if they started it. The police questioned them and my grandparents about it."

"You think they had something to do with it?"

Abby was truly curious and had doubts their dads were on *the up and up* about their past.

"It sure looks that way. I hate to say it, but I wouldn't be surprised if they even started the fire, since they can be dicks."

"Levi! They're our dads! We have to give them the benefit of the doubt on this. We can talk to them when they get home."

"Remember, we have something creepy to deal with. I hope they get back sooner rather than later. They have been known to extend their lake trips, you know?"

"True. We can try to figure this out before they get home though."

Levi was looking through the few articles that were written at the time. He went back to the photo of the burned home and noticed something odd. It appeared that there were shadows in the trees beyond the home that once was.

"Hey Abby, come here and look at this."

She walked around the desk to get a look at the computer. She peered over his shoulder to get a better look.

"What am I looking for? I don't see anything strange."

Levi sighed and rolled his eyes, getting frustrated.

"Look in the trees in the photo. Here." He pointed to the wooded area with the shadows.

"Oh damn, Levi. I really didn't see that the first time I looked at it. It looks like two kids. The ghost isn't a child though. You think they're all connected?"

"No idea. Maybe the ghost lady will tell us." Levi responded sarcastically.

Abby shot him a warning look.

"Hey, Father, you think you have time to go to my house now? Bless my home and look at the black stuff left on the floor?" Abby asked, hoping for a yes.

Father Marcum was thoughtful in his response. "I can. Are you wanting to go tonight? You two can crash here and we can go in the morning if that works for you?"

"Father, with all due respect, I think the sooner we can go, the less time the entity will have to spread her evil in my house."

"I understand. You need to understand that the spirit world is more active at night. I can't promise that we won't encounter the hostile spirit."

"Okay. After Levi is done with his research, we can go."

"Fine. That gives me time to gather some things for the blessings."

Father Marcum looked at Abby and nodded with a half-smile. He approached the door and stated, "I'll need the two of you to refill your empty water bottles with holy water and keep them, just in case." He then left to grab supplies.

Abby and Levi looked at each other, trying to keep their fear at bay, and then continued to peruse the internet for stories about people at the lake at the time of the fire. They still couldn't place who the ghost woman was when she was alive.

"Ah! Look, look at this! Around the same time as the fire where the two kids died, a day later they found a dead woman in the woods. How much do you wanna bet that woman was their mom? Maybe she set the fire and then took her own life? It's possible, right?" Levi looked hopefully at Abby.

"Well, it seems like it would fit. Hand me your water bottle, I'm going to fill them up."

Abby took both empty water bottles and walked to find the fountain of holy water she needed. The church was cold and drafty. She wondered if there were open windows or a door propped open. She made it to the lobby where the holy water fountain was. She filled up the bottles, screwed on the lids tight, and stepped back to head toward Marcum's office. She still was surprised that he was a priest. He didn't seem like the religious type back in high school. Flickering slightly, a few of the lights around the perimeter of the church were going off and on as she walked past them. Above her head, the pot lights were flickering at a steady pace until a couple of them popped, shattered, and rained down over Abby's head. She bent over, covering her head for a moment, then jogged back to Father Marcum's office in the darkened church. As she was reaching for the closed door to the office, she felt a cold burning slap against her hand, preventing her from opening the door.

"Ouch!"

Abby looked at her hand that was still stinging. and noticed the slap marks with two distinctive finger imprints on her skin. Feeling cold all over, she began to shake as the hallway became so cold, ice began to form on the floors and crept toward her from all angles. The lights were playing a symphony of multiple flickers with darkness and light alternating between them. Abby's breath was visible and something slashed through her breath as she snapped out of the trance she felt taking over her thoughts. She never felt more isolated than she did at that moment. Her skin was freezing to the touch, ice crystals were forming on her eyelashes, and her skin was slightly damp with a light blue hue, the color of the sky on a clear day.

In front of her stood what used to be a woman, but now was only a shadow of what she once was. She wore a tattered brown skirt that fell to her ankles. It was ripped along the seams at the bottom. Her top was a worn black v neck sweater that fell to her waist. Mussed up brown hair fell around her shoulders in waves. Eyes black as night that ripped through Abby's soul stared at her while she continued to freeze like Medusa's victims turned to stone; Abby was turning to ice.

Peeking from down the hallway, Father Marcum was caught off guard by the ominous activity in front of his office; in his own church. He stood there, slack jawed and dumbfounded. Realizing what was before him, he quickened his pace, he emphatically held up his Bible and began to yell a prayer as he closed in the distance between himself and the evil before him.

"Saint Michael the Archangel, defend us in battle! Be our protection against the wickedness and snares of the devil! May God rebuke him, we humbly pray; And do thou O Prince of the Heavenly Host, by the power of God, thrust into Hell Satan and all evil spirits who wander through the world for the ruin of souls!"

Father Marcum was standing directly in front of the ghostly woman and Abby, continuously spraying holy water on them with one hand and holding the Bible up with his rosary in the other, repeating the prayer. Beads of sweat began to appear on his forehead and roll down the sides of his face as the Holy Spirit worked through him. Even though the hallway remained freezing, the sweat covered his body underneath his clergy collar and cassock.

"Be gone spirit!"

Father Marcum's voice boomed, and he grabbed Abby, opened his office door, and shoved her in. He closed the door between them quickly. He turned to face the ghost, but the ghost slowly dissipated in front of him, along with the icy floor and walls. He let out a slow, deep sigh of relief. He opened his office door and walked inside and shut it again. He leaned against it and looked at Abby, ensuring she was okay.

"Levi, Abby, how are you both doing? The ghost is gone, for now. We should get going if you still want me to bless your house, Abby."

Abby nodded her head yes, since words had escaped her like the heat from her body. She was still cold to the touch. Levi ran to her when she fell into the office and has held her since. He was rubbing her arms and hands to get the color and warmth back into her body. Staring into her eyes, he felt fearful that she wouldn't be *okay* ever again.

"We need to go. Pick up the bottles of water that fell to the floor in the hallway. I'll drive us."

Father Marcum waited for them to get their belongings and they all stepped out into the hallway. Father locked the office door and headed toward the back parking lot, where his Parish home and car were located.

The darkness had Abby and Levi on edge. Too many shadows for things to hide in and not enough places for them to escape to. A drizzle began shortly after they were walking across the parking lot to Father Marcum's car. The wind picked up as the rain did, spitting drops on their heads and soaking them nearly immediately. The spring temperatures dropped and it was drastically cooler outside. That morning it was a warm spring day with hope and possibilities; now darkness enveloped the innocent with an evil icy grasp. Abby and Levi followed

Father Marcum in a sprint to his car to evade the rain as quickly as possible. They piled in and Father Marcum started his car.

"You both ready for this? Let's just pray that it's uneventful." Father Marcum said as he backed out of the parking lot.

IT WAS A QUIET CAR RIDE TO ABBY'S HOME. Silence remained until they pulled into the circle drive-way. The three of them exited the car at once, slammed the doors shut, and headed to the front door. Levi and Abby held hands and Father Marcum trailed behind. Abby punched in the key code to open the front door. She pushed the double doors open wide.

Father Marcum stumbled back. The air was oppressive and thick with rot. It emanated from the inside out.

"What the hell?" Levi said. "Oh, sorry." Looking at Father Marcum, he gave him a half smile.

"What has happened in my house?" Abby asked, exasperated.

"Evil has happened, Abby." Father Marcum replied

Father held up his Bible and began his prayers while

sprinkling holy water, praying for the safety of Abby and her family, and to protect the home in general from evil spirits. He moved from room to room on the main level repeating the same prayers and sprinkling the holy water a little more than usual for blessings. Levi and Abby followed close behind. When it was time to walk up the stairs, the sulphur and rotting smell of flesh became stronger with each step they took toward the expanse of the upstairs hallway. The smells only became more potent, which proved difficult to breathe as they drew closer to Abby's bedroom; which was clearly the source of the atrocity that assaulted their senses.

Black sludge had grown to cover most of Abby's bedroom floor. Tentacled veins with raven tones stretched and pulsed across the dark cherry wooden floor. Where there were holes in the sludge, the wood had given way to rot. Steam escaped the sludge and dissipated into thin air. Resembling what the depth of an inferno must inhabit, the darkness slowly ate away at the natural light from the wall of windows. The overhead chandelier began to flicker like the lights did in the church earlier. The shadows in the corners of the bedroom seemed to pulse with the lights flaring and vibrations could be felt underneath their feet. Rumblings like a train could be heard from a distance, but sounded closer by the second. Standing there in the doorway, the three of them took in everything before them, then each other.

In the middle of the bedroom, the ghostly figure appeared, wearing agitation like a form fitting dress. She slowly opened her mouth and more black sludge escaped. Her eyes were empty with an endless depth. Her arms hung limply at her sides with thin nearly translucent legs that barely held up her frame. Her long gray hair lay flat against her head, which had a dent on the back right side. A matted spot with old congealed blood clung to her skull, and wisps of hair around the head injury proved her death was a violent one. A large spider crawled from the black abyss that was the ghostly figure's mouth and skittered down her body and hid underneath the bed. The ghost's mouth remained open and she let out a terrifying screech that shook the windows and shattered the glass lights in the chandelier above.

Abby and Levi squeezed their eyes shut and held their hands over their ears when the ghost began to scream.

Father Marcum held up a cross in front of his face, clutching his Bible behind it, while emphatically sprinkling holy water in the hallway before he approached the threshold to the bedroom. Fear was plastered on Levi's and Abby's faces as they cautiously stayed behind Father.

"Stay behind me. If the demon gets too close to you,

douse the demon with the holy water, not sprinkle. Understand?" Looking at them both for confirmation.

They nodded in agreement.

Levi spoke up first. "Demon? I thought it was just a ghost?"

"Yeah, I'm confused here too, Marcum." Abby said.

"A ghost is a spirit from a person that has died and they don't typically harm people. A demon is from Hell and has ill intent towards the living. This is no ghost. I'm sorry, but a demon has attached itself to you both and this is definitely above my paygrade, if you will. I'll do what I can, but I'm not making any promises." Father Marcum entered the doorway and crept a little closer to the demon.

Father Marcum had now garnered the attention of the demon who was making every effort to stand its ground against the priest. It opened its mouth and hissed at him. Father Marcum began praying over the demon in hopes of it going away. Abby and Levi remained in the hallway. Suddenly, the door slammed shut, and the priest was alone in the bedroom with the demon.

Abby ran to the door and tried to open it to see if she could save her friend. She slammed her fists against the door and screamed Marcum's name. Her hands were turning as red as her face, due to the frustration of not being able to get in.

"Abby move over, I got this." Levi kicked at the door several times and finally broke the door, damaging the frame. He kicked it open to an unimaginable scene.

Abby gasped and let out a muffled cry. Marcum was pinned against the wall, several pulsing black roots had taken shape and had twisted around the priest and secured him in a way where there was no escape. One in particular was lodged in his throat. His eyes had rolled back and there was no indication that he was aware she was even there. Movement near her bed averted her eyes, and the large black spider with glowing orange eyes skittered to the priest. It slowly ascended up his body, cresting at his head, covering his face. Abby shook out some holy water onto the dark roots that have covered the entire bedroom floor, making it impossible to walk inside. The roots sizzled where the water hit, which caused them to writhe in what looked like pain. The demon looked at her and hissed. The demon lifted her arm up and spoke in a language Abby did not understand. She became paralyzed with fear and rooted to where she stood. The demon invaded her thoughts and showed her an image from a time before she was born.

A cabin stood isolated in the woods, with other homes being built around it. Two young siblings, (school aged,) were playing inside alone. Two teen boys were nearby at a self made fire pit roasting marshmallows and talking. They were close to the back of the cabin and not paying attention to the wind that picked up and carried burning embers to the nearby home. The fire wasn't noticeable at first. The boys looked behind them and saw that the small home was engulfed in flames. They quickly covered their campfire and ran in the opposite direction. When they arrived at their own lake home, they vowed to never speak of this. Then they found out two younger kids were killed in the fire that was of their doing, albeit accidentally. They took a vow of silence and never spoke of what happened, not even to the police when they were questioned. The police suspected, but couldn't prove anything. It was over thirty years ago when cell phones and home security systems weren't common. The boys' faces looked familiar to Abby and then it flashed forward to now, but at their lake homes. The men she was shown were her and Levi's fathers.

Abby drew in a breath and opened her eyes. Her priest friend was still in a deadly precarious situation and unable to communicate. She looked around and the demon was nowhere to be found. She glanced toward the hallway and backed out of her bedroom to stand next to Levi.

"Fuck, Levi, that demon thing showed me a vison of our dads when they were younger. They were responsible for the death of the two children that died in the fire! Remember the articles that we saw at the church? They were questioned about it, but lied to the police. They never told anyone. I don't think our moms even know. I still think this demon is connected to it somehow!"

"That's not the news I wanted to hear. While you were in your trance, I found a couple of good knives and a fire extinguisher. I wasn't gone that long, I was going to go in there and get you, promise! I'm sorry."

"It's okay, let's see if we can get to Marcum. I'll spray the spider and you cut the root vine looking things!"

Abby grabbed the fire extinguisher from the hallway floor. Levi moved in front of her and began to cut at the roots that were attached to her wood floor. They made a sizzling sound every thrash he made to get to Abby's childhood friend. Not noticing before, she saw that in front of her window, a tree had made its way into her bedroom and rooted itself there, which explained the tree roots that covered the floor. The demon was leaning against the tree, blending in with the shadows and darkness..

Levi made his way to Marcum, and Abby was next to him. She sprayed the spider and it reared back like a bucking bronco and jumped toward Abby. She was able to spray it before it landed on her, and it skittered over to the tree and climbed up, sitting in wait. Cutting the roots that held Father Marcum in place and then the one that snaked down his throat proved difficult. He fell to the floor after Levi cut him loose. Abby and Levi grabbed him and pulled him out into the hallway. He was unconscious on the carpeted hallway floor. Abby shook him and yelled out his name multiple times. Finally, he began to cough. She and Levi turned him on his side so he could cough up the disgusting phlegm that was in his throat.

"Marcum, can you talk? Can you tell us what happened when the door was shut?" Abby asked.

Weakly, he whispered, "When the demon shut the door, she was able to slam me against the wall. I expected something of that nature actually. She didn't like my prayers and holy water and needed me to stop. We need to figure out what demon it is to be able to stop it. You think it's connected to the fire your dads started as kids?"

"What was the date of the fire?" Abby asked Levi.

"I think the thirty-year anniversary was recent, like when we were there at the lake. The lady that was found dead close to that time was their mom. I think the demon inhabited her before she died is my guess. Can a demon lay dormant in a dead body? That's what I want to know."

Levi looked to Father Marcum for the answers.

"A demon needs a live host, not a dead one. That can't be the children's mom if she died before the possession."

"So, the ghost we saw, is a different entity from what's in there?" Levi asked.

"Yes." Father Marcum answered, sitting up and leaning against the wall in the hallway. He needed more time to recover. He was sweating profusely, nauseous from a massive tree root shoved down his throat, and exhausted in general.

Father Marcum had an opinion though, and felt compelled to share it. He took a drink of holy water to wet his parched throat.

"If it were me. I wouldn't return to the lake houses. There seems to be a connection there somehow. But, it seems rather a sinister area. Avoid it."

"Marcum," Abby started, "That's impossible since our parents have lake homes there that they own.

"It's just my opinion, take it or leave it." Father Marcum said.

Abby and Levi grew quiet. Suddenly, the bedroom door flew open. An unfamiliar voice boomed from the dark and brooding bedroom.

"Abby...I'm here waiting for you. Come inside." The demon called.

"What's your name, demon?" Abby asked in a shaky voice. She knew it could sense her fear. It probably thrives on it, she thought.

"Why do you want to know my name? Are you interested in getting to know me?" The demon cackled.

"No, of course not, we want you gone. What's your name though?" Abby asked.

"Well, have you heard of Beelzebub? I'm here to live a life of luxury, like you do. I'm waiting for your dad, any idea when he will be here?"

Father Marcum stood up, even though he was still feeling a bit weak, he grabbed his Bible, rosary, and the remainder of the holy water and took a deep breath.

"Ah, welcome back priest. Want to play again? It's so *fun*." She hissed.

Father Marcum responded calmly, "I want you to leave us alone."

He began to recite prayers and spray holy water on the tree roots before he inched closer to the demon. The demon was clearly uncomfortable and began to hiss at Father Marcum. The roots were writhing on the floor and regenerating at a rapid rate. The sizzling and the smoke rising from the roots was a small distraction to what Beelzebub had in store. The demon was biding his time in the body of a female until he could get a new host. Holding out for a stronger host was vital for the demon to survive. The bodies wear out quickly, so a new host had to be found before the death of the current one.

Levi and Abby were trying to figure out how to help

Father Marcum as he approached the demon. They grabbed the bottles of water that had very little water left in them. They whispered a plan to each other. Getting behind Father Marcum, they wanted to provide backup for him. They just didn't tell him what that plan was.

Father Marcum started his prayers and threw holy water again. Levi and Abby were behind him, like earlier. As he was praying and holding his Bible up, they were following through on their devised plan. Father was creeping up slowly toward the demon and Levi and Abby were on either side of the priest. They ran up and threw all of the holy water on the demon and watched it sizzle and hiss in anger. The priest moved closer and was more emphatic in his prayers and holding his cross in front of him.

Levi pulled a lighter from his front pocket and lit the tree where the spider was waiting. The flames ignited and started to burn, but the demon put out the fire shortly after it started. Levi began to run toward the door where Abby was standing, but the demon didn't let him join her. His arms quickly rose and he began its demonic chants. Slowly, Levi levitated several inches above the floor. He couldn't move, his limbs were paralyzed, and his eyes were wild. Slamming him against the floor, then the wall, the demon was enjoying Levi not being able to free himself from the unimaginable Hell it was putting him through. Levi was then thrown on the bed. He was secured by the tree roots that slithered up the box springs, the mattress, and the roots circled tightly around his limbs. The demon moved over toward him and bent down so its face was parallel to Levi's, nearly touching. Dripping from its face was a mixture of sweat, blood, and black sludge, that landed on Levi's face. Slithering into his mouth, the sludge worked its way down Levi's throat. Choking, then dry heaving, Levi lost consciousness, much in the same way Father Marcum did earlier.

The demon then spoke to Abby. "Bring your father to me. We have unfinished business. I might let your boyfriend live, if you get your father here soon."

"What? How do you know my father? Why are you here?" Abby was barely audible.

Crying and completely inconsolable, she looked to her friend, Father Marcum.

"Abby. I'm so sorry. I'm just not built to handle something of this magnitude."

He hung his head in despair, covered his face with his hands, rubbed his face, then ran his hands through his hair. He sighed deeply and turned his head to look at Abby. He had an empathetic expression, and his eyes reflected sadness from deep within his soul.

"I'm just, ju — sorry. Where are your parents?"

"Levi talked to his parents earlier and the four of

them should be here anytime. I doubt they would extend the trip without telling us. This isn't exactly the welcome home they will be expecting though."

"The only thing I can think of is the fact that there is power in numbers. If your parents and the two of us join together in prayer to defeat the demon, it might work. That's all I got. Well, and a little holy water left. Actually, Abby, can you get more bottles of water? I can bless them and that will work."

"Yes, I'll be right back!"

Happy to be useful, Abby ran down the stairs to grab a few bottles of water from the kitchen. She heard a noise at the front door and went to check things out, setting down the water bottles she grabbed from the fridge. She hurriedly went to the front door and opened it. Her parents were there.

"Hi honey, so happy to see you! Give mom a big hug!"

"Mom, I can't right now, sorry. Shit is happening upstairs. I'll fill you in when you go upstairs. Gotta go get some water blessed!"

"Abby! What is going on? Abby! Abby!" She stared after her for a moment and set all her stuff down.

Abby's parents looked confused and they did not understand what was going on. Her dad started to go upstairs and looked back at his wife.

"Well, what are you waiting for? Let's see what the Hell is going on upstairs."

They both followed Abby up the steps, at a slower, more cautious pace.

Abby ran back toward the kitchen to get the bottles of water and bounded up the stairs to her friend, Father Marcum. She handed the water over to him. He blessed the water bottles with a quick prayer. He knew what prayers he would say in rotation in hopes of defeating the demon and freeing Levi at the same time. He worked his way up to standing, squared his shoulders, and breathed in deeply. He crossed the safety of the sinister threshold and boldly moved forward again toward the demon, to stake claim on this world, in hopes to put the demon back where he came from.

"Hello *priest*." His voice lingered on the last syllable. "Join us." The demon was still hovering over Levi. Running his fingers across his mouth and down his chest.

Father Marcum was stunned. Beelzebub was in his true form. He shed the female ghostly form and opted for his true identity. The devil was here.

Father Marcum began reciting The Lord's Prayer in hopes of preventing the demon from entering Levi's body.

"Our Father which art in heaven, hallowed be thy name, thy kingdom come —"

"What the fuck is going on here?" Abby's dad was at the doorway and looked inside his daughter's room. Fear was plastered across his face and trickled down his spine while he became frozen in terror.

"Ah, just who I've been waiting for. Come closer. We have unfinished business, remember?" The demon spoke to Abby's dad, Chris.

Chris spoke to him, but his tone and volume were weak.

"No, we don't have anything to do with each other!" Chris's voice faltered, giving way to his hidden secrets.

Chris noticed a crumpled female body on the floor by the bed. The demon took notice.

"Oh, her. She ran her course. She didn't last long either. I need a new body to inhabit. I thought about yours, but I think Levi's will last longer." The demon laughed as he spoke to Chris.

"No, please. Leave him alone. He is innocent, he has nothing to do with this!" Chris yelled.

Abby was flabbergasted at the exchange between her dad and the demon, like they knew each other.

"Dad? What's happening? I'm scared." Abby said.

Her mom, Violet, was behind her, holding her back

and just as scared and confused about what was happening as her daughter.

Violet spoke directly to Chris. "Would you tell me what the hell is going on here?"

"Violet. It happened a long time ago when I was a teenager. You remember the fire that killed the two young kids our parents told us about at the lake? Grant and I were cooking marshmallows at a little campfire we made. The wind picked up and embers from the fire blew on the cabin, causing it to go up in flames. We were too close to that cabin, but didn't realize it until too late. That same weekend this demon pops up and promises me wealth and an envious life, plus with the added bonus of keeping it quiet how the fire was my fault. All I had to do was give him a soul. Mine or *someone else's.* I chose the latter. The kid's mom was in the woods walking around, muttering to herself. She was mumbling about a new cabin build for the kids.. I led the demon to her. She was the best I could do without sacrificing myself. I thought she could join her kids in the afterlife. It made sense to me. I guess he had been in her all this time. She was a really young mom, not even 21. It was shitty. But so is that demon over there. *Pure evil.*"

Violet and Abby looked at him with disgust and disbelief.

"I'm so sorry. I wouldn't do something like that now,

you have to believe me! I was 18!" Chris pleaded with the women in his life.

Father Marcum continued on with the Lord's Prayer. He could tell the demon was having difficulty surviving long without a host.

"Oh Levi, we will have so much fun together." The demon cooed to Levi.

"Ow! What the —" The demon was hit with holy water on his face. He was visibly angry and out for revenge. Chris beat him to it.

Chris lunged for the demon to take him down. The demon didn't expect it or anticipate it, and they fell to the floor. The tree roots rolled back toward the giant tree in the corner to give the demon more space. In doing that, the tree roots that had been holding Levi loosened their grip. Father Marcum grabbed him to save him like he helped him earlier. They struggled to get to the hallway, but managed to barely make it before the bedroom door slammed shut.

INSIDE THE BEDROOM, THE DEMON AND CHRIS struggled. Getting on top of Chris and straddling him like a horse to find a position to immobilize Chris proved to be a moderate struggle for the demon.

"Chrisssss. I've been waiting so long for this. You knew this was coming." He spoke with thick sarcasm and condemnation.

"No. Please no. I have a family!"

"I promise to take extra good care of them. Especially that pretty daughter of yours." The demon cooed.

The demon turned to black wretched smoke and entered Chris's mouth. His body shuddered and he screamed in agony. Father Marcum banged on the door to be let in. The door was already broken, but the power of the demon was keeping it closed. Suddenly a ghostly female figure appeared next to Levi. She screamed.

Chris's body was now inhabited by the demon and he slowly looked at the ghostly woman in surprise. Without warning, she entered Chris' body as well. He convulsed and shook uncontrollably until the priest was able to slam open the bedroom door. There was a war inside of Chris, and Father Marcum was unclear how to determine if a Heavenly outcome was even possible.

Again, Father Marcum began reciting his prayers, and this time, he doused Chris with holy water multiple times reciting The Lord's Prayer, louder each time. Chris began to have seizures and couldn't control his own body. By this time, all the tree roots that covered the floor retreated back toward the giant tree in the corner by the window.

Soon, after several prayers and all the holy water was gone, Father Marcum was nearly given out and felt defeated. He sighed and slumped his shoulders and was about to walk away. Chris gasped as a cloud of black dust escaped his mouth and left particles covering his cracked and peeled lips. A lingering wisp of the ghostly entity finally separated itself from Chris and stood next to Father Marcum. She looked kind and reached out to gently caress Chris's face and touch Father Marcum on the arm. She faded away slowly like Chris' last heartbeat.

AFTERWORD

Thank you for reading my collection of short stories. Please consider leaving a review wherever you review what you read. If you enjoyed it, feel free to tag me.

If you or someone you love have been a victim of nursing home abuse, please contact the nursing home abuse hotline at 1-800-677-1116.

If you or someone you love have been a victim of sexual assault, please consider reporting it and the help line is 1-800-656-4673 or chat online at online.rainn.org.

POSSIBLE TRIGGERS:

Implied Sexual Assault in prologue of Clara Knows Possession

CHILD DEATH IN:

Clara Knows Possession
    A Horror in the Dark Woods

Acknowledgments

I would like to thank my sweet husband Matt and my beautiful daughters for putting up with my constantly working and not having much time for the fun things. Thank you friends and family that are so supportive, I couldn't remain grounded and sane without you. Special thanks to Christy Aldridge with Grim Poppy Designs for your amazing cover and interior art! Thanks a million to Meriah Gutterson with Marked Up Editing for putting up with my crazy schedule and demands, you are a gem. I would be remiss if I didn't take a moment to thank Matt Rayner for his friendship and patience. Answering so many writing questions and giving me valuable feedback on everything author related, I truly appreciate all your help. Thank you Andrea and Sara for letting me vent to you about all the things, you both are amazing. To my Scribes group, I adore you all and you know who you are. To the Rayner Patreon group, I love you all. You are the most unhinged fun that is out there and consider you all my ride or die partners in crime (allegedly). To the readers that consumed the pages of this collection, I thank you from the bottom of my heart.

About the Author

Kristal Shanahan writes spooky stories late at night with coffee in hand and music in her ears. If she isn't encouraging her dogs and cat to play nice, she's spending time with her family. Kristal enjoys reading and writing in several horror tropes, mostly everything is palatable for her to read and write. Her credits include a story in *Book Nerds' Book Review 1 (Community Anthology)*, a story in *Scorned Anthology,* and self published independent stories; *Fiery Mable, Clara Knows Possession, and A Twisted Malevolent Christmas.* She also has a story in

Crumpled the anthology. Summer 2025, she will release her debut novella, *Waves of Evil Descent.* Kristal plans to keep writing for the unforeseeable future with numerous current projects in the works.

Connect with Kristal here:

facebook.com/Kristal-Shanahan-Author

instagram.com/LadyinHorror_Author

tiktok.com/@ladyinhorrorwriting

www.ingramcontent.com/pod-product-compliance
Lightning Source LLC
Chambersburg PA
CBHW060353310726
48976CB00003B/803